THE DIARY OF A SOCIAL BUTTERFLY

Moni Mohsin is the author of two previous books, *The End of Innocence* and *Duty Free*, which was read on BBC Radio 4's Book at Bedtime by Meera Syal. Born in Pakistan, she lives in the UK.

MONI MOHSIN

The Diary of a
Social Butterfly

VINTAGE BOOKS
London

Published by Vintage 2013

2 4 6 8 10 9 7 5 3 1

First published by Random House India in 2009

First published in Great Britain in 2013 by
Vintage

Vintage
Random House, 20 Vauxhall Bridge Road,
London SW1V 2SA

www.vintage-books.co.uk

Addresses for companies within The Random House Group Limited
can be found at: www.randomhouse.co.uk/offices.htm

The Random House Group Limited Reg. No. 954009

A CIP catalogue record for this book
is available from the British Library

ISBN 9780099572732

The Random House Group Limited supports the Forest
Stewardship Council® (FSC®), the leading international forest-certification
organisation. Our books carrying the FSC label are printed on
FSC®-certified paper. FSC is the only forest-certification scheme
supported by the leading environmental organisations, including
Greenpeace. Our paper procurement policy can be found at
www.randomhouse.co.uk/environment

Typeset in Fairfield LH by Palimpsest Book Production Limited,
Falkirk, Stirlingshire

Printed and bound by CPI Group (UK) Ltd, Croydon, CR0 4YY

For Faizi, my very own Kulchoo

Introduction

What? What do you mean, 'who am I?' If you don't know me then all I can say is that you must be some loser from outer space. *Everyone* knows me. All of Lahore, all of Karachi, all of Isloo – oh for God's sake, Islamabad – half of Dubai, half of London and all those nice bearers at Delhi's Imperial Hotel also. But since you seem to be an outer-space-*wallah*, I'll ignore your ignorance this one time only, and tell you about me.

I live in Lahore, Pakistan. In a big, fat house with a big, fat garden in a locality called Gulberg, which is where all the well-offs from good baggrounds live. And don't listen to the newly rich cheapsters who live in Defence and say that 'No, no, Defence is Lahore's best locality,' because they are liars. They are just jay – jealous! Anyways, we have ten servants – cook, bearer, two maids (one Filipina and one *desi*, meaning local), two drivers, sweeper, gardener, and two guards who both carry Kalashnikovs, wear khaki uniforms and play Ludo around the clock at the gate. All of these people look after me, Janoo – *uff Allah*, my *husband* – and our son, Kulchoo.

Kulchoo is thirteen (or is it fourteen?). Anyways, his voice is becoming horse and yesterday I was noticing he needs threading on his upper lips. He likes doing something called Wee and reads lots of Facebooks. Naturally, Kulchoo goes to Aitchison College, which is Lahore's best school for nice rich boys from nice rich families. Janoo also went to Aitchison and from there only he went to Oxford in London, and from there he came back three years later, an Oxen. I shouldn't be saying this, because he is my husband and you are total stranger, but Janoo is very bore. He likes bore things like reading-sheading, watching documentaries and building schools in his stinky old village. Did I tell you Janoo is landed? Well, he is. But unfortunately his lands are not in Gulberg, where everyone could see them and be jay. They are a hundred miles away in a bore village called Sharkpur, which I haven't been to, thanks God, for nearly four years. Lots of poor types live there.

Janoo's mother is a widow and I call her The Old Bag. She is fat, bossy, wears flat shoes with rubber souls and can't speak English. But thanks God a hundred million times, she doesn't live with us. Janoo has two sisters – The Gruesome Twosome. They are big copycats and always trying to do competition with me, poor things. Not that anyone can do competition with me. Mummy (that's my mother) says I'm unique.

I am very sophisty, smart and socialist. No ball, no party, no dinner, no coffee morning, no funeral, no GT – *uff*, now I have to explain GT to you also? Get Together, okay? – is complete without me. Naturally, if you are going to be so socialist you also need the right wardrope and the right looks. So I have to get my designer clothes and visit my beauty therapists and my jewellers, and so on and so fourth. Just my selfless little way of supporting Pakistan's struggling economy. Unlike Janoo, who is dead bore, I am very gay. I love travelling – to Dubai, to Singapore, to Harrods and to Macy's – and watching top films like *Pretty Woman* and *Jub We Met* and reading *Hello* and *Vogue* and people's sections of all the newspapers.

My bagground is not landed, thanks God. My family's Lahori through and through. I am convent-educated and afterwards I went to Kinnaird College, where all the rich illegible girls go while they are waiting to be snapped up by rich families with only sons. My family, needless to say, is very sophisty. Daddy worked for a multinationalist company and Mummy was his co-operate wife. Mummy's favourite cousin sister is

Aunty Pussy. She is Mummy's aunty's daughter. Her husband, Uncle Kaukab, was a tax collector. Anyways, they are, by grace of Allah, very well-to-do, with houses here and there, some of which they admit to and some of which they don't. They have one son called Jonkers, who is die-vorced, and we are now looking for a second wife for him.

My friends are socialists like me. There's Mulloo, Baby, Sunny and Nina. Most of their husbands are bank defaulters but they are all very religious and upright otherwise. Unfortunately my friends are also always doing competition with me. But I suppose they can't help themselfs. After all, it can't be easy knowing me . . .

The Butterfly
Lahore, June 2008

January 2001

Haw, such a big scandal in our group, *na*! Tonky's wife, Floozie, has run off with his best friend, Boxer, who is married to Floozie's best friend, Dodie. Just look! What a *tamasha*. Everybody is talking about it at weddings, funerals, parties, everywhere. Floozie's name is mud. Worse than mud. Mud mixed with cow potty and straw, like the pheasants in Janoo's village use to make their houses.

Floozie's name nobody is taking now, except to do gossip of course which everyone is doing full time. Mulloo *tau* has announced to everyone that her doors are closed to Floozie forever till doomsday. As Mulloo so rightly points out, if she can do that to her best friend what will she do to her best enemas? But really, just look at Floozie. She's known Dodie since KG, when they used to sit next to each other in Little Sweet Hearts School on Jail Road only. Imagine! What a snake in the grass she's turned out to be. Back-stabber.

No one is talking about Boxer, though. At least not that much. Because men *tau* are like this only. Everyone knows. Can't help themselves, *na*, poor things. That's why also all the girls, Baby, Nina, Mulloo, Sunny, they're holding tight to their husbands. Their husbands may be bore, they may be crack, they may be fat, they may be ugly, they may be ancient and decrepid, they may be misers even, but it's better than them running off with some racy little number and the whole world feeling sorry for you. And also wondering what's wrong with you.

But going back to poor Tonky. Between you, me and the four walls, the poor thing's always been a crashing bore. Goes on and on about price of wheat – they have lands near Sheikhupura only – and his pesty sides, and his lawsuits, and his heart problems. He was triple by-passed only two years ago and since then he'd grown so careful, *na*, wouldn't even climb stairs, had moved downstairs into guest bedroom, leaving Floozie upstairs in case he got breathless and all.

I would've thought that after twenty years of marriage, Floozie must have got used to. But I should've guessed that something was up when she started getting liposeduction done on her bottoms and her chins, and started wearing see-through clothes in winter also. After looking like an ayah for all this time, why would she suddenly change into a vamp, overnight, if not to lassoo a man, hmm?

Poor old Tonky. He came to our house last night looking like I don't know what. Unshaven, food stains on his shirt, dandruff on his jacket.

Janoo tried to comfort him in his own sour way. 'The best revenge on a man who runs off with your wife,' he said, 'is to let him keep her.'

Tonky laughed like a hyena but there was a mad gleam in his eye. I think so he's going to have a nervous breakout. I told him to go on Prozac immediately. In fact while he was sitting with us only, I sent the driver to the chemists and told him to bring six packs of it. (Thanks God we don't live in London and New York and all where you have to get conscriptions for medicines from doctors.) Tonky took the pills home but now I'm worried that what if he overdouses? I wonder what happens to you if you take a whole pack of Prozac at once only? Do you die laughing?

But look at Boxer. He's sixty if he's a day. Mummy says when she got married he already had broken-down voice and stubbly chin, so big he was then. At her wedding he ran around squirting people with a water pistol and making nuisance of himself. He hasn't changed. Still running around with his hair transplant, his leather jacket and tight jeans – so tight that every time he bends down to pick up something, his face turns purple and his eyes look as if they're going to pop out of his head. Must be male menoapplause. Somebody asked him why he'd run off with his friend's wife.

'What to do? My marriage was empty.'

Crack. As if marriages are teapots, empty or full.

This shows you should never trust anyone. Not best friends, not husbands, not anyone. Except your plastic surgeon and your tailor.

February 2001

Uff Allah, I'm so excited, so excited that don't even ask. Why? *Haw*, on which planet are you living? Apollo thirteen? Don't you know about Basant? There too they must be knowing, I'm hundred per cent sure. How can they *not* know, when all of Karachi and all of Isloo comes to Lahore to attend the kite-flying festival? When everyone dresses in yellow and parties morning, noon and night? Bet they've got their satter-light dishes or cable or whatever it is that they have on Apollo thirteen fixed on all the fun in Lahore also. After all, everybody who is everybody dissents on Lahore. The party groupies Chinna and Bunty and Muddy *tau* always come, but now even serious political types are coming in doves as well. I can't name names just yet, but wait and see on the day and then tell me if I was wrong.

We've been invited to six parties. First there's the bash at Nevernew Studios; then there's the do on top floor of Rafi Plaza; after that there's the Royal

Fans-*wallahs*' function; and God knows what, what else but finally we'll go to Yusuf Salli's *tamasha* in the Old City. That's a total must, *na*. Particularly this year because a PTV film crew is coming there only. They will be doing interviews with family and close friends. Don't want to sound ungrateful but it would have been so much nicer if it had been BBC, then whole world could've seen my canary-yellow designer outfit. How women all over the world from China to Chilly would have envied! Anyways, we should do thanks God for PTV. And they, poor things, will also get a break from bore politics.

French polo team is also here these days. One of them is really cute. All curly hair and naughty smile and fat-fat muscles. Not that a respectacle married woman like myself would give him any inviting looks. But you should see the Available Aunties purring in their slinky saris and plunging necklines. As I always say, everyone has their good name in their own hands. Whether you want to look after it like old china or you want to fling it around like a stainless steal frying pan is up to you only. Anyways, then there's the big polo ball given by Rakshi and Bashir. I think so it's going to be in their garden, all eliminated with fairy lights and oil lamps and all. They could easily have it inside also, so many big-big rooms they've got.

So lots of social things are happening. As Janoo says, the roll call of the Good and the Great is about to be taken. I think so he means Basant and parties-sharties. It's getting harder and harder to understand what Janoo means any more. He's started making such elliptic comments. Recently, he's been firing off letters to Gen Mush and Pres Bush about burning of that newspaper, *Frontier Post. Uff*, I said to him, why bother? It's not as if it was your father's paper. Why are you taking it so personally?

He gave me a strange look and said, 'What would you have me do? Go fly a kite?'

I think so he means Basant. Poor thing, doesn't even know it's not this weekend but next. So out of it he is. Then his friends came around – yes, he has two or three, belief it or not – and he told them a joke about Bush, who asked one of his aids why Pakistan and India were fighting over a sweater.

They all burst out laughing and when they stopped, I said, 'Must be expensive sweater from Harrods only.'

Everyone fell silent, even Janoo, who was staring at the floor. I bet he never thought that I could impress everybody like that. He has always underestimated me. That's his problem.

March 2001

Life's so bore. Basant's also over. Soon Muharram's going to start. In case you don't know this much even, Muharram's the Islamic month of morning when no one has any parties or weddings or anything fun. And then summers will come and everyone will go off to London and New York and Swizzerland and then parties-sharties everything will stop. And Lahore will become total bore.

The festival of Bakra Eid came in between, but frankly, it was so bore, so dearie, that I can't even be bothered to write about it. Instead of slaughtering sheeps like all good Muslims do at Bakra Eid, and distributing the meat among the poors, and getting bonus points with Allah, Janoo wanted to send money to charity, to Edhi Foundation or a hospital or something.

'No need to slaughter a *bakra*,' he said.

'I'm sorry,' I said. 'I may be convent-educated and sophisty and everything, but one thing I won't compromise on – Kulchoo stroking the knife before we kill a *bakra* in our backyard. Stops evil eye.'

Janoo sighed and said, 'If you insist. But in that case I'll send the money to my mother in the village and she can have it done there.'

'Never!' I said. 'She'll eat the money and the *bakra* also.'

'Are you accusing my mother of being a cheap embezzler?' he asked.

'No, *ji*, an expensive one. A good *bakra* costs at least fifteen thou.'

So we had a big fight and now I'm not talking to Janoo. And now he's just come into the room, so I'm going to put away my diary and sit here looking hurt and sad until he says sorry from the bottoms of his heart for being himself.

April 2001

Yesterday we did an after-dinner drop-in at some friends. They all started talking about Benazir and Musharraf. Janoo said that there's no substitute for a two-party system.

'Yes,' I said. 'Totally. As long as one party's in the morning and the other in the evening. Otherwise one gets very tired showing face at two-two places in one night.'

Since I'm so clever I think so I should write a book. What shall I call it? I know: *My Urban Fraud*. It'll be about a rich import-export-*wallah*, who's been married thrice, has nine children, dyes his hair, is sixty-five but still has a rambling eye. I fall madly in love with him and marry him, even though he's beaten all his wives before and beats me also. I have four or five children with him while he has affairs with all my friends, does a huge fraud, robs three banks, and runs away with the maid while I'm left on the prayer mat praying. And then I write my book and tell everyone about how I had a horrible mother, horrible sister, horrible friends, went to a horrible school, married a horrible man and had a horrible life but still stayed innocent and trusting and religious.

I was still thinking about it when I went to Bapsi's reading at Crow Eaters Gallery in Lahore. Bapsi? Sidhwa *na*, writer of *Nice Candy Man* and sister of my favourite Uncle Minnoo of Murree Brewery. Everyone listened so carefully to her reading. There and then I decided, I'm also going to be a writer and give readings to which I will invite everyone except the people who have been horrible to me. Now who would that be?

Well, to start with, my nursery teacher who used to make me stand in a corner for calling her a cow. And the aunties who came to check me out for their sons when I was at college but then never proposed. And Mulloo, for not inviting me to her last dinner when she called our whole gang except me. And Baby for copying my dining-room furniture, and Maha for stealing my Filipina, and of course, Janoo's whole family – The Old Bag, The Gruesome Twosome, and their cheapster husbands and cheapster children, for being themselves.

Anyways, to come back to my book, I asked Mummy to give me intro to an old friend of hers who studied at Queen Mary College with her before it was partitioned. She once wrote a book. Lives in India now. Grey hairs in a bun, handloom sari, glasses. Serious, schoolteacher type. She was here for holidays, visiting her old house on Lawrence Road – it's a school now – and visiting her old school, which I don't know is what now.

I asked her what I should write about – 'Story-vory, plot-shlot, please give me some idea *na*, Aunty.'

She peered at me over her bifocals and said, 'Write about something you know.'

Didn't tell Mummy, but I minded her comment. Says, 'Something you know.' As if I know nothing. I know so much, so much that if I start telling, half of Lahore will have to flee Pakistan. Who knows Mulloo's real age, *haan*? She says she's thirty-nine only, but my foot thirty-nine. She's at least forty-five. I know because her waxing woman told me. She's seen her passport. I don't know how, but she has. And who knows how Sunny sneaks out in a Suzuki early in the morning (in case she's recognised in her Merc) and buys her veggies herself from the cheap Sunday market where all the un-well-offs go? And pretending never to shop anywhere but posh shops like Pace and Al-Fatah. Liar. My cook caught her in the market red-handed, haggling like a washerwoman over the onions. I also know where and with whom Dubboo, Nina's husband, went when he said he was off to Mecca to say thank you to Allah for his new flower mill where he makes hole meal bread. His travel agent is Mummy's third cousin's niece and she told me he got two business-class tickets to Dubai and made booking in name of Mr and Mrs D. Khan at the Joomera Beach Hotel Complex. One room only. Double. With jacuzzi. So don't tell me I don't know anything. Luckily for everyone, I'm too nice to say . . .

May 2001

Guess what? The Old Bag has gone and had a heart attack! Last night only, while Janoo and I were sitting in the lounge, eating strawberries and watching TV, the phone rings and who should it be but one of The Gruesome Twosome, Janoo's younger sister Saika. (I call her 'Psycho'.)

'Ammi's going,' she wailed like a mad dog howling at the moon. 'Tell Bhaijaan.'

I said, 'Bhaijaan's busy watching TV and in any case, where's she going?'

Psycho howled louder and louder until I couldn't hear a word of TV, so I put the phone down and reached for the strawberries.

'Who was that?' Janoo asked.

'Nobody,' I replied. 'Only Psycho.'

'You mean *Saika*,' he said. 'What was she saying?'

'Nothing,' I said. 'Only that your mother's going.'

'Going where?'

I shrugged. Just then, stuppid phone rang again. This time Janoo picked up.

I was lying back on the sofa licking strawberry juice from my fingers when his colour flew out of his face and he started shouting into the phone, 'When? Where? How?'

Then he banged the phone down, turned to me and announced, 'Ammi's had a heart attack!'

'Must be gas,' I muttered. She's always leaking gas, like an old boiler.

'Get up!' he snapped. 'We're leaving for her house right now.'

'At least let me finish this programme,' I protested. 'He's just three questions short of a *crore*. And the servants will eat all the strawberries if I—'

Janoo didn't even let me finish the sentence. 'Come on!' he snapped. As if I was his servant or something.

You can imagine the rest. We sped off to The Old Bag's house with him muttering away.

'I'll have to take her to London. I'll fly her out tomorrow. Book her into the Cromwell Hospital. I'll call Dr Khalid Hameed. There's bound to be a direct flight tomorrow.'

Between you, me and the four walls, my blood really boiled. Here I am begging every summers to go to London, and all The Old Bag has to do is get gas and she's flown out immediately. And probably biz class too. Fat cow.

'What's wrong with Akram Complexed Hospital next to the Gulberg Drain?' I asked. 'She'll feel so at home on the Gulberg Drain. And anyways, I think so you're gushing to conclusions here. No offence but heart attacks happen only to those who have hearts, I mean caring types like me. Mummy always said that when food went bad in the fridge I never allowed it to be thrown away, even as a child. I always gave it to the servants and insisted they eat it there and then, so caring I was . . .'

Anyways, we got to The Old Bag's house and there she was lying on her bed like a collapsed hippo with her eyes shut and muttering, *'Hai, hai.'* Her legs were being pressed by The Gruesome Twosome and all her three maids. The minute they saw Janoo they all started bawling like Bollywood film extras on a death scene. The Old Bag immediately sat up and grabbed Janoo's hand and, with tears pouring down her face, started banging on about her 'dying moments' and her 'last wishes'. I couldn't help noticing, however, that respite claiming to have had a heart attack she still hadn't taken off her heavy gold bangles. They were still jammed on to her fat wrists. I swear, what a *tamasha*! And so bore also. I *tau* sat down on the sofa and helped myself to some fruit. Nice plums, but not as nice as at Mummy's house.

Doctor came and did a check-up and then he asked her about her signs and systems. Apparently The Old Bag had been feeling some tightness in her chest. And breathlessness also. Naturally. If she will wear her shirts so tight what does she expect? All she had to do was to let out some seams and darts in her poplin shirts but no, she had to go and fake a heart attack. Anyways, doctor took Janoo aside while I was having my third plum and told him that she'd had a vagina attack.

'See,' I said, 'it's only vagina, not heart.'

'Angina,' Janoo said loudly.

As if I'm deaf or something. This is the thanks I get for abandoning my TV and my strawberries.

June 2001

You know, you can tell about people in one minute flat. Who is from good bagground and who is not. Now look at Princess Salimah Aga Khan, who visited Lahore a couple of months back. She is real Princess and all, you know, but sooo humble, sooo understated that don't even ask. I met her at a dinner and you know what? She didn't even wear a crown. This is being from good bagground.

And then there's Jonkers' new crush: Miss Shaheen, his secretary, who is a slippery little number if ever I saw one. The way she's managed to get her sharp little nails into Jonkers is nobody's business. Appearing so sweet and gentle from the outside while being a total gold-dogger on the inside. And Jonkers, loser, fool, stuppid, he fell for her, book, line and sinker.

He calls me a thousand times a day and sings her praises – Miss Shaheen this, Miss Shaheen that. I swear my years have got exhausted. 'She's so respect-able, so hard-working, so thrifty, so nice.'

So finally I *tau* told him: 'Jonkers,' I said, 'listen to me. You are son of Pussy Khilafat, grandson of Mr Khilafat, great-grandson of um, um . . . Mr Khilafat Senior, great-great-grandson of Mr Khilafat Very Senior. How can you marry a nobody?'

'She isn't a nobody,' he protested, his eyes shining dimly like twenty-what bulbs behind his inch-thick glasses. 'She is Miss Shaheen and she is also somebody's daughter and somebody else's granddaughter and great-granddaughter.'

'Oh, for God's sake, she's not somebody's granddaughter, she is nobody's granddaughter.'

'How can you be so snobbish?' he asked.

'Same way as you can be so stuppid,' I replied. 'She is after your money. And the minute she gets it, she'll be off like a bullet from a Kalashnikov. You wait and see. And anyways, if she's so marvellous, why don't you introduce her to your mother? *Haan?* Why do you keep calling me, expecting me to do your dirty work for you? Persuading Aunty Pussy and all, *haan?* I'm telling you from now only, someone with a name like Miss Shaheen can only be a gold-dogger.'

'She's not!' said Jonkers and put down the phone.

Honestly! this Jonkers has always been such a problem. So stuppid he is. So gullable. So trusting. Always falling for the wrong types with tight-tight shirts and lose-lose morals. There was that Aqeela, the hairdresser – actually not even hairdresser, blow-dryer – whom Aunty Pussy paid two *lakhs* to and got rid off. Mummy and I used to call her Akela, the lone wolf. Then there was Typhoon, the telephone receptionist who said 'foon' instead of phone, and wore too much powder and too little deodorant. I was sure Aunty Pussy would trump Miss Shaheen's card in no time, so I wasn't very bothered. After all, Aunty Pussy isn't known as 'Pussy the Past Mistress' for nothing.

The next day while I was still in bed, phone rang. It was Aunty Pussy screaming herself historical. 'That fool! That bloody damn fool!' she shrieked. 'He's brought this – this woman to my house who is a *secretary*. A *secretary*! And he has the gall to introduce her to me as his wife-to-be. *His wife-to-be!* I was so shocked, I dropped my teacup. Thank *God* it wasn't my Rosenthal.'

'Miss Shaheen?' I breathed.

'You *know* her? You know about her? You *know* that he's planning to marry her and you haven't breathed a word?'

'He never said he was going to run off, Aunty Pussy. Just that he had a crush. I thought it would pass, like malaria, you know. I *tau* even refused to meet her. I could tell from her name only what she would be like. Is she like that?'

'Worse!' wailed Aunty Pussy. 'Much, much worse. She calls jam "jem" and she ate an omlette with a teaspoon! What shall I do-hoo-hoo?'

'You should change your locker at the bank and hide the key. And you should take Jonkers' name off your house and put it in your own again. And you should pack away your good shawls and your silver. And then, you should pray.'

God help Aunty Pussy.

July 2001

I tell you, these shawl-*wallahs*, they're the limit also. Last week this smooth-talking type came with his bundle on the back of his motorbike. Wanted to sell me a shawl, a *jamawar*. Big-big paisleys with orange boarder. Asked for two *lakhs*.

Now, I'm fine with *shahtooshes* and things. In fact, I have four – one beige, one green, one brown and one navy-blue-and-grey rewindable. But *jamawars* are just so bulky, *na*, that I feel as if I'm wearing a duvet. So I was about to send the shawl-*wallah* off when I remembered that all my coffee party crowd have *jamawars*. Mulloo, even. Apparently, they shout old money.

'How much?' I asked.

'Three *lakhs*,' he said. 'It's over a hundred years old. It's an unteek Begum Sahiba. Unteek.'

'Antique-shantique nothing,' I said. 'One *lakh*. Not another *paisa*.'

'One *lakh* seventy-five.'

'One-twenty.'

'One-seventy.'

We argued for an hour but he wouldn't budge. So stubborn, these people are. And so greedy also. Fight over every last *paisa*. Then I thought, forget it. In any case summers are here and I won't get to wear this shawl for another seven months at least, so why should I let him eat my head for nothing?

'*Bus*,' I said. 'I've decided. You give me the shawl for one-twenty and that's final.'

So he said, 'Let's not argue about money. Why don't you keep the shawl overnight and think about it?'

He'd just left when Mulloo called. '*Hai*, I'm so excited,' she said.

'Why?' I asked.

'I've fallen in love with a shawl, a really old antique *jamawar* with huge paisleys and this lovely tangerine-coloured boarder. That crafty Kashmiri came to show it to me because he knows, *na*, that I am very tasteful, so I saw it and straight away fell in love. But I can't afford it because I bought diamond earrings from Carat jewellers last month and Tony will kill me now if I ask for a *jamawar* also, and I got so depress that I was popping three-three Prozacs but then suddenly I remembered the hideous gold bangles and necklace that I got from Tony's family when we married that

I've always hated because they're so *villagey* you know, and so today I went to Carat and asked him to put a price on it and he said it was two *lakhs* so now I'll call the shawl-*wallah* tomorrow and buy the shawl. Will have to haggle a bit but I'm sure he'll give for one-ten. *Hai*, I'm so excited!'

'But don't you feel like you're wearing a duvet when you put on a *jamawar*?' I asked.

'Who wears a *jamawar*, *yaar*?' snorted Mulloo. 'You just drape it off one shoulder. So classy it looks. Seema Iftikhar has such a nice collection. All the old-money types have them like other people have napkins.'

So I put the phone down and immediately called the shawl-*wallah* and handed him one-twenty-five Cash. In crisp thousand-rupee notes. He counted every note, as if I was some kind of lying cheater or something. What happened to trust, to morals, I ask you?

August 2001

Just my luck to be married to a kill-joy. Here I am so gay, so gay that everyone says I'm the sole of the party, and there's Janoo who is more bore than Pal Gore. Really, only I can cope up with him. Anyone else would've die-vorced him long time ago.

Now just look at this. After all those long bore summer months of no action, there was one grand wedding, oho of the Kasuris. You know, him a minister and she a multimillionaire businesswoman. Their youngest son was getting married. Three-week-long celebrations, food to die for, air-conned marquee that accommodates two thousand people, anyone who's everyone, from ex-presidents and ambassadors to fashion models and society hairdressers. Only people missing were the leaders of our two biggest political parties, Benazir Bhutto and Nawaz Sharif. Oh I forgot, they're both in exile.

Anyways, instead of being happy that he'd been invited to such a big socialight wedding, Janoo refused to go.

32

Crack. Said he liked the Kasuris very much but found weddings boring. He said, just listen to this, that he'd go after the wedding and wish them in peace and quiet.

'But they haven't invited you to wish them in peace and quiet, they've invited you to a wedding,' I explained in that slow voice doctors use for cracks on TV. 'Tomorrow our child will be getting married and what will happen if everyone turns up after the wedding to wish us? Hmm? I'll tell you what will happen. Our marquee will be empty, our driveaway will have owls hooting, our food will lie uneaten and will have to be distributed at Data Sahib's shrine among the poors, and my shweetoo Kulchoo will receive not a single envelope bulging with cash and there'll be no fun and no dancing and no society photos and no video-*wallahs*. No one will compare notes on what a fab wedding it was. No one will copy the bride's outfit. No one will goss about the past-it clothes the in-laws wore. No one will ooh and aah over the jewellery I wore, and no one will come and say, "Honestly, only you could have organised such a fab wedding." You know what will happen at Kulchoo's wedding? Nothing. Because no one will come. Our noses will be cut and our faces will be blackened. That's what will happen.'

'Ah,' said Janoo, putting down his papers, 'that would be most unfortunate. Most unfortunate indeed! Twenty years hence, Kulchoo will have a small, unremarkable wedding because of my regrettable lack of social skills. But fear not, my dear. I may be a social disaster but luckily you have yourself to rely on. The indefatigable socialight who hasn't missed a single function of a single wedding in the sixteen years that we've been married. Thanks to your heroic efforts we can count on at least 5,000 people turning up at our son's wedding. So, really, there's no fear of having to feed the homeless at Data Sahib.'

At that I decided, I damn care. Let him be a loser if he wants, I'm *tau* going. So I put on my latest designer outfit, the red satin with gold sequence, and hung in my years Mummy's ruby earrings, the ones that fall to my shoulders, with matching necklace and solitary ring, and off I went.

First person I bumped into was Pooky, Janoo's cousin sister, who'd tucked the sides of her *hijab* behind her years to show off her massive emerald earrings. So cheap she looked. So obvious. She stared pointedly at my diamond solitary ring, which I was wearing on my right hand, and said, 'Isn't that the wrong finger?'

'Isn't Janoo the wrong man?' I replied. Why should I stay quiet? She gave me a sour look and pounced off.

But I also didn't let her stuppid comments spoil my fun. I went up to everyone and said at least 800 hellos.

Some of them, for instant Asma Jehangir, the human rights lawyer – the guests to whom I said hello – I hadn't seen for months. And others I hadn't seen ever. Frankly, the ones I didn't know looked a little startled, but I smiled brightly and said how nice they looked and how nice it was to see them and now I really must go because I must mix up with the other guests also. I wonder if they thought I was crack? Never mind. Let them think whatever they want. After all, I'm not doing it for myself. I'm doing this just for Kulchoo.

September 2001

All this time I've been living quietly with Janoo, but if ever there was a time to leave him, it's now. I swear, he spends his whole life in front of BBC and CNN, sometimes only he'll switch to Star News. And our stuppid cable is also fixed so that on channel 53 it's CNN, on 54 Star News and on 55 BBC. One stuppid news finishes, another stuppid news starts. Can Kulchoo and me ever switch to sensible channels like MTV or B4U or AXN? Never in a million years. *Bus*, Janoo's hooked onto this America versus Talibans drama. I said to Janoo, What's so interesting now? Twin Towers have gone, Pantagone has gone, please switch to B4U. He ignores me and sticks to bore BBC.

Yesterday, I *tau* let him have it. 'If anyone should be upset, it should be me. After all, Aunty Pussy, Mummy and me were planning a trip to New York and Mummy's third cousin was coming to Pakistan, leaving her apartment and cat for us to look after for two whole weeks. Mummy'd said that Pussy'll look

36

after the cat because she herself is quite catty. And then this planes-shlanes and Twin Towers thing goes and happens. Worst timing. Why couldn't they have waited for another two weeks? I could have gone and come back from New York.'

Mummy says Masood has done it – Twin Towers, what else? Apparently, Masood is the Israeli intelligent agency that does lots of bad things all over the world.

'Why's it called Masood?' I asked Mummy.

She said, 'You don't know, darling, these Jews, they're very clever. They've given their secret servants a Muslim name so that everyone thinks it's us who's doing all the hanky-panky everywhere.'

Look at them, I swear! Mummy says on that day, all four thousand Israelis who worked in World Trade Centre were told not to come to work. Masood warned them from before only.

And then some people are saying that Bush had the planes flown into the Twin Towers himself. Why? *Haw*, isn't it obvious? Because he wanted an excuse to evade Afghanistan and then Iraq and then Iran and then Syria and then Sudan and then maybe Saudi also. He wants their oil, *na*. So greedy he is.

But Aunty Pussy, as usual, doesn't agree. She's always liked to be different, from the time when she was a little girl and wore only jodhpurs and ate only okra. Anyways, she says Pal Gore's done it. Bush rigged the election and now Pal Gore's gone and done this so that Bush's guvmunt will fall. And everyone will say, look how incontinent he was!

And just look at the Indians. They're so jay, just because we're best friends with America again. Reminds me of Basheeraan who lives in a shack in the slumps across the canal and used to do my waxing. When I sacked her and hired her neighbour Hameedan, she became so vicious that don't even ask. Just because we've become the Americans' servant again, Indians are doing all sorts of proper-gainda against us on their TV.

But Americans also I don't understand. Sometimes they are saying that we Muslims did it because we are jay of them. Because they live in skyscrappers and condoms and eat Big Macks and hot dogs and watch Jerry Sponger and Opera Winfrey. And they have freedom and we don't.

But darling, who wants to live in a condom, even if it's on a beach in LA, if you have to do your own laundry and cook your own food and wash your own car and even fill your petrol yourself? I mean, is that a life? Honestly! I'd much rather live in my mansion in Gulberg with my cook, drivers, maids, sweeper, bearer, gardener and guards than any old condom in LA. And as for skyscrappers, what if electricity goes, *haan*? Who will climb up and down those fifty floors then? And anyways, I *tau* love my lawn. So nice for parties in winters. And the nice thing about Gulberg is everyone who's everyone lives here. Mummy's just round the corner, Sunny's on my backside, Mulloo's down the road. And because we are so close to the ground, no plane can fly into us . . .

October 2001

I am so depress. Why? Try living with my in-laws. I tell you, one day with them and you'd become suicidal. Yesterday Janoo's younger sister dropped in. There I was having a perfectly nice morning, getting my legs massaged, when suddenly I looked up to find Psycho standing there in her polyester outfit (I wish someone would tell her that polyester is so over), clutching a box of sweets.

'These *gulab jamans* are for you, Bhabi,' she said.

'I don't touch these traditional-type sweets,' I said, waving the box away. 'Too much of sugar, too much of butter, too much of chloroform.'

'You mean cholesterol,' she smiled. 'And never mind, Bhabi, after the way you slog at the gym to shift those few stubborn tons you can afford a little indulgence.'

Bitch. And how dare she talk about my few extra ounces when she herself looks like Marilyn Brando in his last years?

'It's just that I haven't seen one of these boxes for so long,' I purred. '*Mithai* is so last millennium. But maybe it's still trendy in Iqbal Town – or was it Bahaar Town? That's where your cosy little cottage is, *na*? I always get mixed up with all these new-new, little-little developments.'

'My double-storey house is in Defence, actually,' she replied. 'Bilal's just got a new job. Very big job,' she persisted, boasting like the cheapster that she is. 'He now has 200 people under him.'

'Must be mowing the grass in the graveyard, then,' I said, yawning delicately.

'And Bilal's sister's been elected to the National Assembly,' she continued, ignoring my comment. 'We're all going to Isloo in our new Prado jeep for the swearing-in ceremony.'

'The same sister who is four feet tall and hunch-backed?' I asked. 'Or is it the one who is cross-eyed with buck teeth? Anyways, who cares about the election? If I wanted I could win two-two seats tomorrow,' I said.

'Really, Bhabi?' She forced out a laugh. 'And what would be your constituency?'

'Me?' I said. 'I have a bigger constitution than you can even dream of, where I prop up the entire economy with thousands of people dependent on my goodwill.'

'And where's that?' She pretended to smile sweetly.

'Liberty Market, of course,' I replied equally sweetly. 'All of Al-Fatah Store, Kitchen Cuisine, Saleem Fabrics, dry-fruit-*wallah*, Ehsan Chappals, even Book Gallery where I buy my *Vogue* and *Harper's*, they would all die if it were not for me. I would only have to nod at them and they'd come pouring out in their thousands giving me ten-ten votes each.'

Thanks God after that she stormed out, leaving me with my massage woman. I threw the *mithai* to Kulchoo's labradog but afterwards I watched him carefully to see whether he died a slow horrible death. You never know with these jay in-laws . . .

November 2001

Janoo's given me ultimatum. He says he's not going to any parties or any balls or any weddings this winters.

'But why?' I asked.

'Because I don't feel like it.'

'And why you don't feel like?'

'I'm just not in the mood. That's all.'

'And why you are not in the mood?'

'I'm not in the mood because of the war in Afghanistan. I don't have it in me to party at present.'

'But you were being so happy that Talibans were being beaten. You *tau* were clapping and shouting and saying they were running like rabbits. Now you've changed your mind. Become a hippo-crit? Hmm?'

'No, I haven't become a hippo-crit,' he said. 'I'm still delighted that the Taliban are being ousted, but I don't like to see Afghanistan being bombed yet again.'

'So they should have thought of that, before inviting Osama to be their house guest, no?'

'I don't think ordinary Afghans had any say in that.'

'But ordinary Afghans can have say in whether we go to parties or not?'

'Oh, for God's sake!' muttered Janoo. 'I don't know why I even bother trying to explain things to you.'

'Because you are so bore that no one else wants to listen to you!' I shot back. 'And I also only listen because I'm forced to.'

So Janoo took a deep breath and said quietly, 'I don't want to party while Rome burns.'

Rome? Are they bombing Rome? Has Osama run there now? *Haw*. No one even told me. Now I suppose Janoo won't want to go out because of Italians. If you ask me, I think so he's trying to find excuses. In fact, the more I think, the more I think so that maybe he doesn't like parties.

December 2001

Just look at this Mullah Omar. Honestly! What a disappointment, no? How he was leader of Talibans if he was such a coward? Okay, you can't stand so much of bombing but at least you can go into the mountains and become a gorilla like Osama. Instead, he's sneaked off on a motorbike from the middle of a bazaar. And look at the Americans, also! Standing around in the bazaar scratching their heads while he escapes from under their noses in broad daylight. And that also on a scooter! Such losers! And everyone keeps saying they are so clever, so clever they have satter-lights that can read the lines on your palms and tell your future from outer space. Humph! As far as I can tell, they can't even read the number plate of Mullah Omar's scooter. Honestly, you know it's not like me to complain, but I've been so let down.

But, really, Mullah Omar's also blackened our faces in front of the whole world. Even worst, he's blackened my face in front of Janoo. I was so sure, *na*, that Mullah Omar would fight till death like Muscle Crowe in *The Gladiator* that I even made a bet with Janoo, who predicated that the Talibans would scatter like ashes in the wind. I said, some people have more guts than to run, okay? And now look what's happened. I'm feeling so angry, *na*. So let down. The least they could have done was to think about my bet before shaving their beards and scurrying off like clean-shaven rats.

On top, Janoo keeps rubbing it in. 'So, where's your precious Mullah Omar now?' he asks, grinning from year to year.

Uff, at times like these I just can't take him. So irritating he is. Gets on my nerves so much. First *tau* I kept listening quietly. But then I also let him have it.

'When I married you,' I said, 'I thought I'd found Mr Right. I would have thought a hundred-hundred times before saying yes if I'd known your first name was "Always".'

January 2002

I wish the year was full of Decembers and Januarys and Februarys. No more bore Junes, Julys and Augusts, when nothing happens except the monsoons and the floods. All-year parties-sharties, balls-valls, weddings-sheddings, return of all the abroad-*wallahs*, constant GTs, new clothes, comings and goings – *hai*, how nice that would be. This year *tau* the winters have been totally fab.

First there was the Sindh Club Ball at Sindh Club only. What a fantastic do, I tell you. Fifteen hundred people and each one best of the best. Hussain – oho, Haroon – Abbas Sarfaraz, Salman and Sally, Irum and Irshad, Faiza and Fussy, and my friend from America, Topsy and her sister Turvy. And Gulgee, Sherry and Nadeem and the Rehmatullahs – basically, anyone who's everyone was there. I enjoyed dancing to all those Indian Bollywood numbers so much, so much that don't even ask. I think so the only person who didn't enjoy was bore Janoo, but then what's new?

All evening he sat scowling into his glass. I asked him what his problem was. He said, 'Here we are on the verge of war with India, and everyone's dancing away as if it was a bright new dawn,' and he drained his glass in one gulp.

Frankly speaking, I really don't know what to do with Janoo now. Maybe I should send him to a shrimp. But I shouldn't say anything in front of him in case he minds. Even though he's bore, I still have to keep on the bright side of him because the Lady Duffering Ball is still to come and I have to drag him to it. As it is, getting him to go to the Sindh Club Ball was like getting Bush to go on a picnic with Osama. I shouldn't say but Janoo's become such a stuttering block in the path of my social life. Anyways, let me tell you about this fab party in Lahore that I went to.

Organised by Jalal – Salahuddin, *na* – at Isbah's house only. Three hundred people in, and 500 out on the waiting list, shivering in the foggy cold. Felt so good walking past all those shivering hopefuls with my nose in the hair. Inside it was even more amazing, with all those thin-thin models in their little-little clothes and high-high heels. And all the silver-haired uncles lounging around on sofas watching them dance from under lowered lids. And the blonde, botoxed aunties watching their uncles-husbands like Batman watches the Joker. Bar was flowing full time. And platters of sushi going past. I tried a sushi but it tasted all raw-raw. I think so they'd forgotten to cook it. So when nobody was looking I quickly spat it out into a bush, wiped my mouth, reapplied my lipstick – MAC's Russian Red – and teetered off to the dance floor on my six-inch heels. So much action. I wish January would last the whole year. Without the fog, but.

February 2002

'I think so my best month is February,' I told Janoo as we were driving to Sunny and Akbar's for dinner. 'I used to think that December is my best, but February is most best.'

'I agree. There's something uplifting about spring,' he said.

'Particularly the springs of a Merc, they are the most uplifting,' I said, wondering how we'd got on to topic of car suspenses. Sometimes I think Janoo's becoming sterile. 'Pajero is also okay, but I think so maybe Prado is better.'

'I meant spring, as in season. You know, blossoms and flowers and birds and barmy weather?' sighed Janoo.

So that's why he was talking of springs. He's not totally crack, thanks God.

'For me spring is only Basant,' I replied. '*Uff*, I can't wait. The whole week is going to be wall-to-wall functions. I'll be going to so many parties that I won't even have time to say hello to anyone.'

Janoo gave me a funny-type look, but just at that moment we arrived at Sunny and Akbar's so I didn't have to ask that why you are giving me such funny-funny looks?

Dinner wasn't too bad. It was on the small side. About thirty people only. Half inside, half outside. Some sitting in sitting room, some lounging in lounge, some, as Janoo said, inhaling grass on the grass. I think so he meant the scents of springs and the smell of new grass and so on and so fourth. Food was from Avari, although Sunny pretended her cook had done it. Liar. I've ordered those fat-fat, fried-fried prawns myself so many times. And not to mention the cold slaw and the smoked salman and the chocolate mouse. All from there only. Honestly, I don't know why people have to lie, particularly when they know they're going to be found out. Also pretended she'd done the flowers herself, when I know she'd stolen the arrangements from that charity dinner yesterday. I saw her with my own eyes only, sneaking off with the centre arrangement hidden under her fake pashmina shawl when she thought no one was looking. So much of lies. So much of reception.

Anyways, talk was all about the coming parties. Janoo says a lot of the Basant parties will be coke-fuelled. I think so because Coke must sponsoring, *na*. They and Emirates. God bless for making so many deserving people happy. Also, Razzak Dawood's son is tying the string. The wedding will be in Karachi and Lahore over a whole week. We're sure to get invited because Janoo knows him from before. Must remind Janoo to call him and just do hello-hi to refresh his mammaries. And then Imran Khan is having a fund-raiser with Amitabh Bachan in his hospital. I wish he'd asked Shahrukh Khan. Amitabh is also not bad, but now poor thing has become a bit aged. After all, he was a hero in Bollywood back in the '70s and '80s. When I was a tiny little baby.

March 2002

Mummy telephoned early this morning, about twelve-ish, while I was still in bed, to tell me that Uncle PJ had gone.

'Gone where?' I yawned.

'To Him.'

'To whom?'

'*Him.*'

'Who's he?'

'Oho, God. Him. Allah.'

'Oh *Him,*' I said. 'Why didn't you say so?'

'I said so.'

'No, you didn't.'

'I did.'

'Didn't.'

'*Did!*' she shouted. 'For God's sake, stop arguing.'

I was about to slam the phone down when I realised what she had said.

'You mean he's dead?' I asked.

'Yes.'

'*Haw, hai,*' I said. 'How? When?'

'Last night in his sleep.'

'Poor thing! So that means he didn't find out until the morning, when he tried to wake up but couldn't.'

'Something like that.'

'But we mustn't be too sad,' I said to Mummy. 'He lived to a respectacle age, thrice married, seven children, two grandchildren, lived a very full-up life. I think so he must've been eighty at least. When was his birthday?'

'July 15th,' she said.

'Which year?' I asked.

'Every year,' she said.

'No, Mummy. I mean, when was Uncle PJ's birthday?'

Again she said, 'July 15th.'

'But which *year*, Mummy?'

'I've *told* you, *na*, every year,' she said. 'Except next year.'

Poor Mummy, she's become sterile. Everything she forgets.

Anyways, now we have to do the funeral and burial, because Uncle PJ had fought with his last wife and all his children. Not that he's left anything to us. Shouldn't say bad things about dear departeds but he was such a miser, such a miser that don't even ask. Mummy says everything of Uncle Pansy's is in

a numbered account in Swizzerland. His paintings –
he had twenty-five miniatures – he'd also put there.
He'd even sold his carpets and his silver. No one
knows the number of his account because, God bless
him, he was so miserable. He didn't even trust
Mummy, his real cousin sister, with the number.
She says it's probably four-two-zero. I think so it's
zero-zero-seven, because Uncle PJ liked to keep
secrets. But honestly, least he could have done was
to give Mummy the keys of his locker in Swizzerland
so she could pay for his funeral. It's not fair, *na*, to
expect others to pay. Like we'll have to now. Or else
everyone will talk.

Anyways, Uncle PJ, however miserly he may have
been in other ways, was quite considerate in some
ways. I mean, he could've died before the LRBT Ball,
but he didn't. Or he could've died during Basant even,
but he didn't. Instead he died in Muharram after
finish of party-wedding season and before start of
London season. So we didn't have to cancel anything.
Thanks God.

But I still wonder where the account is and who
knows the number. Someone must be knowing. I've
heard sometimes people give numbers of their birth-
days for their accounts and things. What did Mummy
say was Uncle PJ's? Oh yes, July 15th. So that's 15.

And July's six. Or is it seven? Now what's the rest? I think so I better call Mummy and ask.

'Hello? Mummy? You know Uncle PJ? When was his birthday?'

'July 15th.'

'But what year?'

'Every year. How many times do I have to tell you?'

'But when was he *born*? What *year*? Hello, Mummy, are you there? You said once that he was seven years older than you. What year were you born?'

There was silence on the other end.

'Mummy? Can you hear me? What year were you born? Tell, *na*, Mummy, because I think so I might be able to find his numbered account that way.'

'I can't hear, darling, line's gone all fuzzy.'

Strange, I thought, I can hear her as clearly as if she was sitting opposite me.

'Mummy,' I shouted. 'What year were you born?'

'*Uff*, darling, it's hopeless. Can't hear a thing. I'll have to ring off. Byeeee.'

April 2002

I'm so fed up of servants and their crooked ways. So much of lies they tell, and so much of rubbish they talk. Constantly trying to pull the wool over our flies.

Now look at my sweepress. On Monday she took a day off. Just like that. When she rolled in on Tuesday, bold as Brasso, I asked, 'Why you didn't come yesterday, *haan*?'

'Because Musharrat had borrowed for himself the minibus I take from Dharampura to Gulberg,' she replied.

'Why would Musharraf need your minibus?' I asked. 'Doesn't he have a hundred-hundred Mercs to ride in?'

'For his rally at Iqbal Park,' she replied. 'All the buses, minibuses and even the tractor trolleys they took for Musharrat's rally.' (I don't know why these illitreds keep calling him Musharrat instead of Musharraf. I think so they confuse him with Musarrat, as in Musarrat Shaheen the actress.)

'Who took?' But before she could answer, I said, 'All

lies! I'm going to throw you out because you are a liar. *And* you came late.'

'But, Bibi,' she wailed, 'I'm not lying. I swear on my dead mother's head.'

And then they do so much of drama also.

'The same mother who died three times last year, and for whose every death you took ten days off? That mother?' I asked.

But just imagine, the cheeks! Now I know for a fact that Musharraf came to Lahore by helicopter, which landed in Iqbal Park itself. It said so in the news, even. Which crack would take a sweepress' minibus when he had a helicopter at his disposable?

So I told her very quietly that I was deeply disappointed in her attempts to befool me and the one thing, the *only* thing, that I wouldn't tolerate was liars and schemers. And she should be ashamed of herself after everything I had done for her, giving her ten days off every time her mother died and not even cutting her days off from her celery as Baby or Mulloo would have, and not even deducing the cost of the cut-glass vase that she broke last month, which my sister-in-law had given to me. (Actually, I'd always hated that hideous thing that Janoo's horrid sister Cobra – okay, okay, Kubra – had brought for me from Jeddah and was sooo reliefed when it finally broke, but of course

I wasn't about to tell the sweepress.) So I said to her that I was a good, kind-hearted sole, whose only fault was that I was too good and kind-hearted and so everybody takes my advantage, but I have my limits also and enough is enough, and with that I kicked her out. You have to take a stand with these people, *na*, otherwise they take walks all over you.

When I tried to tell Janoo about it next morning, he completely ignored me, so busy he was with his newspaper reading bore-bore things about Musharraf's Preferendum.

Anyways, when finally Janoo put down the paper, I told him about my principaled stand with the sweepress.

'She was probably telling the truth. Didn't you know that Musharraf's toady district councillors had confiscated all public transport for the day? So they could bus in their constituents to Musharraf's historic rally? You should read the papers sometimes,' he said.

It was on the trip of my tongue to say that, 'I watch so much of Fox TV but there was no mention, no nothing of Preferendum and minibuses in it, and then I thought, forget it. It will only lead to more arguments.

Next day when I woke up at my usual eleven o'clock and saw the house, I noticed that it was beginning to look dirty with so much of dust everywhere. So I sent a message to the sweepress to say that I'd forgiven her, because I was a good, kind-hearted sole and she could come back. Let's see, now, whether she comes. Problem is, I spoil my servants too much.

May 2002

I had such a lovely time in Murree. Janoo's Oxbridge society had a GT (oho, how many times I have to tell you, Get Together) at Saigol Lodge in Murree. Everyone came. First there was golf, then lunch, and then most best, goss. I was sitting there with my sunblock on and my shawl pulled over my face – to guard against a tan *na* because in mountains the sun is very strong – and chatting to Ayesha and Farah, when I felt my chair shake.

'*Hai Allah*, earthquake!' I shrieked.

Ayesha, who was applying her lipstick, looked up briefly from her compact.

'Don't worry, even if it is an earthquake, it'll only affect the poor parts of town. Earthquakes are very considerate that way.'

'But what if it's a bomb?' asked Farah. 'Bobo says war can break out any day with India.'

I heard this and all the colour flew out of my face. All this time I've been telling Janoo that come let's go to London early this year. Why do we have to stay here and take all this tension-vension when we could be in Shelfridges enjoying their Bollywood Season and meeting Amitabh and drooling over Dimple's bedroom, which Baby told me (she's just come back from London and all) has been flown out whole and soul from Bombay only. Imagine, seeing the bed she sleeps in and the table she sits on to do her make-up! Also, they've got all those designers like Rohit Ball and Shyam Someone. And all the clothes that Hrithik Roshan and Kajol and my favourite shweetoo darling, Shahrukh, wore in their films. But Janoo refuses to go.

'I'm not deserting my country in its hour of need,' he said flatly.

'And what about my hour of need?' I replied. 'My Dr Seebag cream is gone, my YSL Rogue Eclair is finished, my La Perla bras have become loose – size, thanks God, is still same but elastic's gone – and my shoes are looking so last year.'

Janoo looked at me as if I'd gone mad.

'Does it not matter to you in the slightest that we may be on the verge of a nuclear war?' he asked.

'Of course it matters,' I said. 'That's why I'm saying let's go. Why would I want to stay here and become a *suttee* when I'm not even Hindu?'

'I'll build you a bunker in the back garden,' he said,

shaking his head. 'You can sit there and apply your make-up every day, while war planes zoom overhead.'

'I'm not going in any bunker which doesn't have air-con and generator and cable TV and three-three phone lines and marble bathroom and jacuzzi. And I don't want to be tucked away in the back garden where no one can see me. I want to be in the front, by the rockery.'

'In that case you'd better go to London,' Janoo said. 'Kulchoo and I'll be better off without you here.'

'And have everyone say that you are having an affair while my back is turned? And become an object of pity? No, thanks. I'm going to sit here on your head and eat your brains from morning to night, every day, till you agree to come with me.'

June 2002

So much fun I'm having these days. A nephew of mine is visiting from America. His name is Asghar Haq but he's lived so long in Mary's Land in Washington that he calls himself Oscar Hake. His father, Ayub, has big halal meat business there. He's a millionaire I don't know how many times over and that too in dollars, not stuppid rupees. But he wasn't always like that.

When my cousin Minnie got married to Ayub, everybody said, '*Haw*, poor Minnie', because he wasn't from a big city like Karachi or Lahore but bore, backward Gujranwala and he had a small little meat business. Mummy used to call him 'Mayub the butcher'. But what to do, *na*? Minnie was getting quite aged – at least twenty-six – and proposals weren't coming, so her mother married her off so that people wouldn't say, '*Haw*, poor Minnie. She got left overed, *na*.'

But then they migrated to America because his lottery came in American Consulate – in the good old days, before the Americans became all mean and suspicious and stopped giving visas – and there he set up his business. Before we knew it, they'd bought a big house in the suburbs with a swimming pool and landescaped garden and guest house and servants.

Minnie *tau* changed overnight. She used to be quite plumpish and quite shortish. And darkish also. But now she's so thin, spends all her time in the gym and has a personal trainer, and I think so has also had some liposeduction and chemical peal done because her colour has become all creamy-creamy. I don't think so it's just Jolen bleach cream. And she wears killer heels and killer clothes, all designer of course, and looks fab. And of course, Ayub *bhai tau* is sooo nice, *na*. He's invited us all to come and stay. Mummy says she's going first, because she's always respected Ayub *bhai* from the bottoms of her heart.

So I asked Oscar what his mummy was up to these days.

'Mom?' he said, rolling his eyes. 'Aw, she's either playing bridge with some other frustrated housewives or off having her colon irrigated.'

I must tell Janoo to get his crops done the same way. If Minnie's doing it, it must be right.

Anyways, Oscar is sho funny and sho shweet. Calls himself The Dood. I think so he means dud. All the time he's cracking jokes about himself. So self-defecating he is. And so considerate also. Spends hours in his room because I think so he doesn't want to get on our nerves and when he comes out it smells so, so . . . sweet and herby and strange. Like the smell Peshawar bazaars have. And he smiles all the time and speaks slow-slow and looks a little bit on the dumb side, to tell you the truth, with his uncombed greasy hair and his huge, baggy jeans hanging down from his bony hips, as if he'd done potty in them. But I *tau* haven't said even a word in case he minds and then he tells his father and his father takes back his invitation.

Janoo says he's just an ABCD loser. ABCD? *Haw*, don't you know what that means? American-Born Confused *Desi*. But I think so Janoo is just jay because he doesn't have anyone half as rich or half as sophisty as Oscar in his villagey family. So as usual I ignored him.

Shweetoo, Oscar's so worried about the bombs-shombs. So innocent. Just like a foreigner. But how awful that bomb outside the American Consulate in Karachi was. Imagine, poor Sindh Club members playing tennis opposite and suddenly being hit by flying

70

body parts. Thanks God it didn't happen during a party on their famous front lawns.

Must rush. I'm giving a dinner to show off my trendy, rich new nephew to Mulloo, Baby and all. Just to make them jay you know . . .

July 2002

Look at Aunty Pussy, honestly. She's managed to get a visa, not only for London but also a Shagging Visa, which means she can go to France, Spain, Italy, Germany and all. And poor Mummy's been refused. What I want to know is how Aunty Pussy's getting it. I think so she's doing something from inside only. All the while on the outside she pretends to be so innocent.

'*Haw*, you all are not going?' she asked me, knowing fully well that poor Mummy's been refused and I'm reapplying next week. 'I thought they were giving visas out like flowers give out perfume.'

Actually, it's all Mummy's fault. Who told her to go and stand in the cue at the embassy with sunblock, sunglasses and headscarf? Naturally they thought she was a *hijabi* fundo and mistooked her for Al Qaeda. Now, who's going to explain to these polaroid white visa officers that all Mummy was trying to do was avoid a tan?

But, honestly, these stuppids should be given lessons in what's what and who's who in Pakistan before they are posted here. I mean, they should know from just looking at us with our Jimmy Choose shoes and the two-two-carrot diamond studs in our years and our nice fair skin that's never been exposed to sunlight and our nice soft hands that have never washed a plate that we are nice, rich, well-off types from good baggrounds who've been to London hundred-hundred times. We are hardly the types who are going to become runaways in London and get jobs in their crash'n carrys and marry cockney types who live in councillor houses and eat up the state. Nor are we beardo-weirdos who are going to drive planes into their buildings. We are just not the types. But these stuppids in the visa office, they don't even know this much.

But obviously, lots of peoples are getting it even apart from Aunty Pussy. Look at Irum and Amo, Yusuf Salahuddin, Salman Taseer, Sheila Saigol, Raunak Lakhani, Abbas Sarfaraz – all of them going off to Harrods sale. I've *tau* even stopped going to Al-Fatah, in fear that I'll be spotted and pitied for being still stuck up in Lahore when everyone who's everyone's long gone to London and New York for the whole of the summers. Last weekend I sneaked over to Karachi to get all the essentials at Agha's – sunblock, La Prarry products, latest *Vogue*, Hagendaze and Orio cookies for Kulchoo. And guess what? Bumped into Zarmeen, who lives in London and is the only person who comes in the opposite direction in the summers.

Before she could say anything, I said, 'Hi, how are you? I'm only here because I'm flying out from Karachi to London, *na*, rented a flat there, right on the back-side of Albert's Hall.' Luckily, by then it came her turn at the till and I ran off. Just about managed to get into the car before bumping into anyone else.

Can you imagine how my nose will be cut if I don't get the visa now? I'll never be able to show my face in society. How Mulloo will laugh. How Sunny will titter. There's only one solution. If I don't get it, I'll have to go and hide in Sharkpur for a whole month – *uff!* – and pretend that I got a Shagging Visa and went to Berling and Burn where Janoo had some works and we were treated like royalty. I'll never get caught out because nobody ever goes to Berling and Burn . . .

August 2002

Uff! I'm so exhausted *na*, after this three-city tour of that small Indian god, Aruna Dhati Roy, which the TFT-*wallahs* had arranged. But even after three days one thing I still don't know and that's why people keep calling her a small god.

I'll never forgive the organisers. They're such misers they never sent me a card even. First, I tried pulling stings. Aunty Pussy's best friend's son is a district counsellor, and so I called him to ask him to get me the tickets but I think so he must be abroad or something because every time I called, his secretary said he was out. So eventually I just called the organisers myself and said, 'Why aren't you giving me a ticket, *ji*? Don't you know who I am?'

And this small-time receptionist or manager or whoever it was who answered, said, 'Why don't you email in your request like everyone else?' Just look at his guts!

I felt like replying, 'Because I'm not everyone else.'

But then I thought, why do arguing with receptionist types? So I begged Kulchoo to do an email for me.

'What's the point?' he asked. 'You'll never be ready by 2:30 p.m., which is when the event starts.'

Thanks God for Janoo, though. Turns out, he had emailed in his request and got his ticket. Luckily, I saw the card when it arrived. I went barging into the study and said, 'What is this? Going alone, are you? I also want!'

'But you have no interest in writing or politics or activism,' he said.

'Why, *ji*? Don't I have interest in society? Don't I have interest in hotels? In events? In going out and about? Anyone who's anyone will be there. Mulloo's going, Sunny's going, even Mummy's got a ticket. Why should I be left behind?'

So anyways, he filled in the email for me, and where they asked for 'profession', he wrote 'luncher'. I'm least bothered, as long as I get the card.

Just as well I went, because everyone was there. ALL of Lahore. Mummy and Aunty Pussy, Mulloo and Tony, Faiza and Maha, MT and VD, Jonkers, Bobby, Baby, Sunny, Sammy, Nina, everyone. Even Janoo's sisters, The Gruesome Twosome, and their hideous husbands had weasled their way in. Strangely, there were lots of people I didn't know also. Wonder who they were? And how they managed to get in?

It was nice event but problem was there was too much of talking. Long-long, bore-bore questions and long-long, bore-bore answers and long-long, bore-bore speeches and so on and so fourth. Loved Aruna Dhati's sari. Janoo cried when Aruna Dhati finished her speech. So emotionally unstable he is. But thanks God he had the decency to weep silently and not bawl out loud and shame me in front of everyone. But what there was to cry about, I don't know. It was hardly as if someone had died or something.

Anyways, I did my bit of culture. Now I don't have to do anything for another three years.

September 2002

Thanks God a thousand-thousand times that summers are going. I *tau* get so excited when September comes. Have you seen *Come September*? Such a lovely film with Frock Hudson and Gina Laylosomebody. Old, but nice. And made for Pakistan, only. Honestly, this summer was so bad, so bad that don't even ask. Both boiling *and* bore. Small GTs are okay for time pass but they can't take the place of a heavy-duty party. Also, Aruna Dhati and all's coming for the *Friday Times* bash was also all fine, but all said and done, she's a bit serious and a bit bore, no? Between you, me and the four walls, I *tau* was quite disappointed with her. I mean Bookish Prize winner and she wasn't even wearing designer clothes!

Now, look at Danielle Steal. So nice she looks in her soft-focus photos with her big-big diamonds and her high-lit, blow-dried hair. And Barbara Cartland, who was even older than Aunty Pussy, wore her false eyelashes even in her coffin. So vain she was. And it's not as if Aruna Dhati is not pretty or something. She could look quite nice with high heels and ironed, streaked hair and some of YSL's Touché Eclair and Landcomb mascara and MAC lipstick and so on and so fourth. But if she is least bothered, then what can anyone do? I suppose you have to live and let die. But such a waste, no?

Hai, I hope so we can make friends with India. Imagine hopping across to Delhi every time you need a new outfit, or new emerald earrings, or even a new party. Imagine being invited to the Tatas and the Godrejes and ringing up Shobha Day for hello-hi whenever you want. Then maybe even Janoo can get a life instead of sitting in front of the TV all day and watching all this 9/11 drama with a disgusted look on his face. If only he was a committed peacenik like me, he could also be enjoying in Bombay, and running up and down the hills in Gulberg in Kashmir, and buying saris in My Sore. (Mummy says best ones come from there only.)

Peace has other benefits also. I hear servants are soooo much cheaper in India. You give them a 500-rupee tip and they do a thousand *salaam*s or *namaste*s or whatever it is that they do over there. Here *tau* they look as if you've done their insult unless you give at least a thou. I *tau* am thinking of firing all my staff and getting everyone from over there only. Nice-nice Biharis, sweet-sweet Sylhetis. Or are the Sylhetis from Bangladesh? Whatever! As long as they just do what they're told, I don't care who they are or where they come from.

If we become all peaceful, I suppose Kashmiris will also become friendly, no? And then they can start knitting *shahtooshes* again. Price of a decent shawl has gone so high, so high that don't even ask. My shawl-*wallah* told me that it's because the Kashmiris have put down their knitting needles and picked up guns instead. I think so it's very selfish of them, but who listens to anyone these days? Except me. Sometimes I think so I'm the only decent, obedient, God-fearing, law-abiding, kindly, nice, honest person left in the whole world. Me and Mummy.

October 2002

So bore. Nothing's happening. I'm going to sleep till November.

November 2002

Mummy's right. It's a curse to be sensitive. Take me only. So much worrying and anxiety I do that I can't sleep at night. I told Janoo about my sleepless nights.

'Good!' he said. 'Since you are up all night you can keep watch on the house and we can dismiss the guards.'

'Do I look like a servant to you?' I asked. 'And anyways, I refuse to be the only house in Gulberg without security-*wallahs*. People'll think we are either misers or we can't afford it.'

Anyways, to cheer myself up, I went to see Mulloo, who'd just come back from Bangcock. She was sitting in her back veranda, her face covered in bleach cream and her head encased in a helmet of mouldy-green drying henna. I don't think so she was expecting company. Poor thing, she was never pretty but honestly, one shouldn't say, but she looked like an extra from Kulchoo's favourite film, *Star Wars*.

So I clapped my hands, giggled and said, '*Haw*,

Mulloo, you look just like an extra from *Star Wars*!
You know, one of those creatures with a trunk like an
elephant's and three-three eyes and years like palm
fronds and skin like an alligator's.'

Forgot, unlike me Mulloo has no sense of human.
Just can't take a joke *na*. She got so angry that the
cream nearly curdled on her face.

'I'll have you know,' she spluttered, 'that all my son's
friends call me Yummy Mummy.'

I thought to myself that they must be calling her
'*Return of the Mummy*'. But this time I didn't say in
case she bust a blood vessel or something. '*Haw*, but
why have you put bleach cream on your face? It's to
make your skin white like mine?'

Again she hit the ceiling. 'It's for making – no,
keeping – my skin smooth and supple,' she shrieked.
'And if I were you,' she continued, 'I'd buy the whole
factory to keep me in enough cream to erase those
deep trenches around the eyes.'

Look at her! Is this any way to talk? And to someone
who's so sensitive? My hand flew to my face. 'Oh these
tiny, feathery lines?' I laughed. 'These are *tau* only
laughter lines.'

'Nothing is *that* funny,' she snapped.

So I stomped out of her house and called Mummy

and cried my heart out to her. And thanks God I did because Mummy told me that Mulloo has always been jay of me because I've always been the colour of apricots while she, poor thing, no matter what she does, has khaki skin. And anyways, if my little lines bothered me, not that they should because you needed a microscope to see them, but if they did, there was always botox. So I'm ordering two crate-fulls of botox tomorrow. And then I'll see what Yoda says!

December 2002

You know my friend Moni – Moni Qayyum, who's husband is big bureau cat and who runs Begum Boutique. Anyways, Moni was saved personally by Allah. She was coming from London in a plane and as they were driving down the runaway to take off, suddenly there was a loud crash and the whole plane trembled and quivered like a new bride. And then the driver braked hard and told all the passengers that they had to go back because the nose of the plane had fallen off. So the driver (he hadn't become the pilot yet, because the plane hadn't taken off) asked Heathrow Airport if they could give him a new nose and, of course, bore English types being bore English types, they said that they don't do nose jobs and particularly not on a Sunday. So the plane and everyone in it was standed for two days in London. Just imagine, how Pakistan's nose has been well and truly cut by PIA.

But maybe they weren't to blame. I'm sure it must

have been Al Qaeda or even the Indians who shamed us like that. Honestly!

Anyways, I said to Moni, you must say lots of prayers and kill lots of sheep and say many many thanks to Allah because really, you've been saved by the skin of your teats. Imagine what would have happened if the plane's nose had fallen over the sea or something worst. These days I feel so unsafe that I don't even leave the house without reading prayers from the Holy Quran and sprinkling myself and Kulchoo with water that's had prayers said on it. I don't bother with Janoo because he says he is an antagonistic. So why waste my prayers on him? After death I'll go to God and he'll go to Lenin.

But I'm not sure whether even Lenin would bother with him. I hear Lenin's fallen on such hard times himself. Apparently no one even gives this much for him in Russia anymore. Nobody bothers to even read the Bible at his grave. At least they could do church service in his mammaries and sing carols and hims and all. But no, not even that much they are prepared to do. Just look at the Russians, how ungrateful, no? These days they are all busy doing bows in front of that new man, Putting, or is it Yell Skin? Whoever. But I didn't tell poor old Janoo all that because I didn't want to make him depress.

So what else? Nothing much except that balls are coming and by hook or by book, I'm going to the Merry Adelaide one for leprosy or pleurisy or whatever illness it is. See you there, darlings!

January 2003

New Year's was so bore. J&S events-*wallahs* went off to Karachi, and as a consequent there was no big bash in Lahore. All there was were little-little GTs here and there. Azam and Amber had a little dinner, Nuscie and Jeelo had a little dinner, Seema had another little dinner and Ena had yet another little dinner. *Bus*, we went here and there eating little-little dinners and doing hello-hi. I told Janoo I won't rest till at least fifty peoples have seen my new Rizwan Beyg outfit, so we had to party-hop. Janoo kept grumbling but came along because I told him it's New Year's and it comes only once a year and that too right at the end. If I hadn't told him I don't think so he would've known. Also, with what face would I meet Kulchoo next morning if we came home before him?

I belief there was a party at Central Party Head Quarters, a.k.a. Yusuf Salli's house in the Old City where everyone from Mick Jagged to Aamer Khan has been intertained. But it was a children's bash with a few desperate uncles lurking in the shadows scoping out the teenage girls. There was a fab do at Ramzan Sheikh's farm; we were also invited, but Janoo, loser that he is, put his feet down and refused to drive through the fog all the way to Bedian near the Indian boarder at 2 a.m.

And this morning Mummy woke me up with a call at the creak of dawn saying I must go to hospital immediately, because Uncle Kaukab has taken a turn for the worst.

Poor thing! He's Aunty Pussy's husband, *na*, and in his time such a big shot he was. Tax inspector with a big house full of TVs, VCRs, stereos, cars, fridges and servants. He told me once that God helps those who help themselves. And he helped himself for about thirty years to everything that was going. And not even going.

Anyways, when Mush took over and started that accountability drama Uncle Kaukab panicked, quickly sold one house and sent the money abroad. That money Aunty Pussy investigated in a motel in Ontarion started by her cousin. How was she to know that cousin would eat all their money? Then the other house, which they'd put on rent, there the tenant became a swatter and wouldn't pay or leave. Uncle Kaukab threatened the tenant but discovered that although he looked very harmless, with thick glasses and dentures, he was related to a big underworld boss who runs a huge betting business, and he sent his glooms to Uncle's house and they dragged him out into the driveaway and beat the living headlights out of him. Poor thing!

He's in Javed Akram Hospital now, and if he doesn't improve we're putting him in the Aga Khan. It clean skipped my mind that I'd offered to get him two bottles of blood from Janoo's sisters. They don't know yet, but the least those two fat cows can do is give some blood to my poor uncle who's been through so much. I would have given myself only, because after all he needs blue blood, but what to do, I'm so ameanic that I can't even give to an ant.

February 2003

Jonkers was always a problem child. Now he's a problem man. Poor Aunty Pussy is at her split ends. But what to do? Seeing as he's her only son and all. You know *na* that he went and did that marriage of inconvenience with Miss Shumaila, the telephone operator – or was she a secretary? But he is also stuppid and gulliver, I mean gullable. All she had to do was to massage his ego a bit with '*Hai*, so handsome you are, just like a film star', and he was eating out of her grubby little hand with the chipped nail polish. And then she had to swing her polyester-clad hips at him a few times, flatter her eyelashes, and he was ready to sign on the spotted line with her and hand over everything that his father, Uncle Kaukab, had cheated so hard to make and Aunty Pussy had fought so hard to hide.

I told him a hundred-hundred times that Miss Shumaila was a gold-dogger and that she was after his money but would he listen? Screamed and shouted at me and said I was jealous and cyclical and didn't recognise true love when I saw it. After that I didn't say anything because why to get insults for nothing, hmm?

'Total operator she was,' poor Aunty Pussy told Mummy when Shumaila ran away just four months later with all the jewellery and things. Aunty Pussy had tried to hide the jewellery in her safe, but Jonkers brought a pistol and threatened to blow his brains out if she didn't give it to him. I told Aunty that she should have let him. What brains does the poor thing have to blow, after all? But back to Miss Shumaila, she didn't even leave Jonkers' gold cufflings from his shirt. And on top she drove off in the new fully loaded Corolla Salon that Jonkers had gifted to her on the morning after their bridal night.

Now we have to get Jonkers married again. Aunty Pussy hasn't asked me straight out yet but she's been dropping hints like we were in a grand quiz or something . On top, Janoo's no help at all. He keeps asking, 'Has Jonkers met his next ex-wife yet?' I swear, he really needs a tight slap.

Anyways, I told Mummy that she should go and do hand-holding with Aunty Pussy because I *tau* don't want to get involved. But to call me as soon as they'd seen the girl and tell me everything from start to finish.

Not because I'm nosey or anything but because I'm concerned *na*.

So last evening they went to see Aunty Pussy's sister-in-law's cousin's neighbour's daughter, who's slightly darkish. Also, her parents were saying she's twenty-nine, which means she's at least thirty-three. Jonkers also is thirty-seven and die-vorced, but he's a man so it doesn't count. From what all Mummy tells me I think so the darkish girl will work out because, poor things, they're not as effluent as Aunty Pussy and all, and you know how poor people get impressed with money and property and things, *na*.

March 2003

I've shut-upped everybody – The Old Bag, The Gruesome Twosome, Janoo, even Bush and his English sidekick, 'Tony the Phoney' as Janoo calls him. I've shut them up them with my anti-Iraq war demo, which has come on CNN, BBC, even Fox. After all, five thousand women and children marching through Gulberg is no joke. And all rich types from good baggrounds, who are doing it for their principals and not for the hundred rupees the rent-a-crowd types get. Nobody can say after this that we rich Gulberg-*wallahs* don't stand out and speak up – or was it stand up and speak out? Whatever. Everyone's very impress and that's that.

At first I wasn't getting involved. You know, *na*, how I am the shy, retired type. Not at all like those shameless types who are forever pushing themselves forwards for every small thing. And also, just between you, me and the four walls, I thought that the only ones taking part in the demo would be just those ten or twenty handloom NGO types who come out whenever a girl is gang raped or a woman is thrown into prison for not wanting to marry a man chosen for her. I thought they'd be the only ones raising slogans and getting arrested. And honestly, one doesn't want to be lumped with that NGO, activist crowd, *na*, with their undyed hair and their ethnic cloth bags and their un-made-up faces. Because, after all, one is different. But then I went to a coffee party at Mulloo's, and everyone there was discussing who-who was going and it turned out almost everybody who was anybody was. How could I be left out of the social scene? So I immediately pushed myself forwards and said I *tau* all along was wanting to be one with Iraqis.

On the day I sunblocked my face, neck and hands, donned a new cotton outfit (can't wear silk on protest marches, I'm told, it gets very sweaty), put on my new Channel sunglasses with the huge rhinestone Cs, and laced up the bright white Nike boots I'd bought from Al-Fatah the night before. The whole world shook when we marched through Liberty Market raising slogans and posing for TV cameras.

When I got home, I strode into the sitting room triumphantly and announced to Janoo where I'd been. He switched off the BBC, stared at me for ten minutes full and finally asked, 'Why?'

So I glared at him and said with my head held high, 'Because I feel for the Iraqis. That's why.'

'Hmm, interesting,' he said. 'More than you've ever felt for Pakistanis, obviously.' And then he looked at my Nikes and said, 'Marching against American imperialism in your new American shoes, I see? Still, I don't mean to belittle your efforts. Well done.'

Sour lemon.

Only problem is where to go this summers? US is out of question. Poor Bubbly's son, who is at university in Taxes, is having such a tough time that don't even ask. His parents have told him, 'Pretend you've got Larry-gitis so you can't speak at all if anyone asks you whose side you are on.' And Kinky's younger sister, who is in an all-girls' college in Messachewsits, is wearing both a big cross round her neck and a *bindi* on her head, like good Hindu girls, so nobody thinks she's Muslim.

But look at that traitor, Tony! Oho, not Mulloo's husband but Blair. How will we go to London now? Will we even get visas? Honestly, so unfair he is! After all the money we've spent in London on flats-shlats, cars, restaurants, shops and all, least he could do was let us go and enjoy. Our money's welcome but we are not. Now take Bobo and Bunny, you know they spent three million quids on a flat on the backside of someone called Albert Memorial and Bobo bought a Porch, which he keeps parked in a garage there, which is more expensive than monthly rent for a mansion in Cantt – and now they can't even go and use it. And why? Because their passports are green and that's not Tony's favourite colour any more. Just look at that!

April 2003

So bore these weeks are: parties finished, balls finished, life finished. Nothing to keep me going except for a bit of goss here and there. I've heard that MacDolands has changed hands but in Lahore only. I'm planning to rent out the Main Boulevard branch for Kulchoo's birthday party, but I think so I'll have it transferred into a jungle for a Mowgli-themed party. I was telling Mulloo how every Tom, Dick and Hairy has birthday parties in MacDolands (her daughter also had hers there only), and little bit of difference in organisation is a must to extinguish myself from the crowd.

'*Haw,* darling,' purred Mulloo. 'Trust you to think of it. You could switch off the air-cons and make it all hot and sweaty and *junglee*. Then you could also get the management to take the electricity off the bill. What a big saving that will be for you! And instead of going to all the expense of a Kitchen Cuisine cake, you could just plonk a bunch of rotten bananas on the table. And also, Kulchoo can wear a red underwear instead of a decent pair of Ralph Lauren kiddies jeans. But tell me, what are you going to do about the animals? Inflatable ones from Icchra, that down-market bazaar where all the penny-pinchers go?'

'Well,' I replied sweetly. 'You've accepted the invitation, so that's Colonel Haathi sorted out, and your shweetie daughter will take care of King Louis the ape, and Tony is *tau* a natural Kaa the sssnnake. Really, with friends like you all, who needs animals?'

Later I told Janoo and he had a good laugh, but he said not to have the party at MacDolands because their food is not healthy.

'Haven't you read *Fast Food Nation*?' he asked me.

'*Uff!* How many of times do I have to tell you I'm not into cookery books?'

Look at all those clueless MNAs who've gone to India to do talks. Musharraf should have sent me instead. So many heart-to-hearts I would have had with designers and jewellers and sari-sellers and hostesses. After all, that's what they want, no? People-to-people contract? One me could have done the work of all those bumbling parliamentarians.

Instead, I went to the Tariq Ali talk in Lahore with Janoo. Janoo told me it's the first time he's spoken in Lahore since 1969.

'*Haw, tau* all this time he's been whispering?' I asked.

But I wish I'd gone to Furry's coffee party instead. Her sooth-slayer was coming to read the palms of all the girls there. She had predicated that Furry was going to have a surprise visit from someone with very expensive tastes. Furry got all excited thinking Jemima Khan was going to visit her. Instead, her house got burgled that night.

May 2003

God safe me from family. I said it in front of Janoo, and he said that there was a famous English poet or librarian or something – how you can become famous as librarian, God only knows – who also said that families stuck you up. But mine *tau* is really driving me around the bends. Ever since Jonkers' wife, that razor-blade Miss Shumaila, left him, Aunty Pussy's been dropping hints left, right and centre about how he needs to get remarried.

'You must know thousands of girls,' she said to me. 'You know we're not choosy. Anyone will do.'

I thought and thought till I got a my-grain. It's not easy you know. Jonkers, poor thing, he's a real shweetoo and all but he still wears big, fat glasses and safari suits, and that also polyester and one doesn't like to say but he's also not so rich after the Ontarion debuckle. Finally, after much calibration, I suggested someone to Aunty Pussy.

Okay, I accept she's an elderly girl, thirty-two or

whereabouts, but comes from an okay family, not exactly rich but okay. Father was middling-type officer at Shells or Uni-Leavers, or maybe ICI even. Anyways, it was multinationalist company. Girl went to the Convent. Same as me but there the resemblance ends. She's not a craving beauty or anything, but nice in a simple way. (But then, Jonkers is also not Brad Pitts.) When I suggested her to Aunty Pussy, she hit the ceiling.

'You think my Jonkers is so desperate that he'll marry an aged nobody from nowhere?' she shouted. And then she banged on and on about this girl's problem with her biographical clock.

What the clock had to do with the girl I don't know, but I said, 'Take her clock to Kronos Time Centre on the Mall only. They're expensive but they can fix anything. They even did Daddy's grandfather. Clock, I mean.'

Then I told her that better do the wedding in the summers only, because nobody's getting visa for London so you have a captive audience.

'I'll ask J&S event managers for a nice cut-price theme,' I said. 'For instant, "Sense and Sensibility" would be so appropriate, no?'

Suddenly, Aunty Pussy just lost it. Not over the theme, but the expense.

'What do you think this is?' she yelled. 'The opening of a new hotel?'

'*Haw*, Aunty,' I replied, 'in your times, the olden times I mean, it may have been okay to cook a couple of dishes and do a small ladies-only-type ceremony and that was that. But nowdays you can't even open an envelope, let alone a hotel, without an event manager. Didn't I tell you I had Kulchoo's birthday done by them also?'

At that, she said I could take my marriage proposal and my event managers and my Kronos Time Centre and go to hell. Next time I'll see if my shoe even listens when she moans about her loser son.

June 2003

You know what's happened, *na*? Our neighbours got thieves last night. Promise by God. They came in just before dawn prayer time, tied up the night watchman (they are poorish, you see, not like us who have proper security types with Kalashnikovs and khaki uniforms), herded the whole family, kids-shids, everyone, into the sitting room at gunpoint. And while the family sat quietly and watched, the thieves cleaned them out. Took everything. Computers and DVD and TV and jewellery and silver and all the cash-vash – everything. They even took their mobile phones. Everything they loaded into a van they'd brought, which they'd parked in the drive only. Imagine, right next door to our drive all this was happening.

When they'd finished, the thieves sat down the terrified family and said to them, 'To tell you the truth, we are very disappointed in you as a family.' While they sat there mutely, not daring to breathe, the chief thief says, 'Aren't you going to ask why?'

The father and mother exchanged glances and then the father stammered out, 'W-why?'

So he gestured towards them all with his gun and said, 'Have you looked at the way you're dressed? Specially your daughters? Wearing nighties, and those too, half-sleeved? Haven't you thought how you will look if thieves came to your house? Luckily we are not the kind who will treat you badly or punish you for not being dressed properly in Muslim way, but times are bad these days. You should take more care.'

And then they said goodbye and left.

So today I called Mulloo and told her.

'I *tau* sleep in high-necked, long-sleeved *shalwar kameez* with my *hijab* tied tightly under my chin, and so does my daughter,' she said. 'The thief was absolutely right, times are bad.'

So I charged into Janoo's study and yelled at him that instead of two-two professional guards, I want four-four at night. 'And instead of obsessing about the war on tourism and weapons of mass distraction and Guacamole Bay thousands of miles away, you should be paying more attention to what's going on in your neighbour's house.'

But thanks God I didn't have too big a fight with him, because it expired later that he's just put a down payment on a house in the hills. Now that he refuses to go to London and New York he's buying a house in the hills, finally.

Except that it's not in nice, desirable Nathia Galli where all the rich sophisty types go, but in dull old Changla where no one goes. When I discovered, I hit the fan.

'But the in-crowd is all in Nathia!' I yelled.

'That's precisely why I've bought in Changla Galli,' he smirked.

'How did you find anything in Godfortaken Changla?' I asked.

'Serendipity,' he said.

'Who's she?' I screamed.

'No one you are ever likely to know,' he replied.

Must be some cheapster like Jonkers' Miss Shumaila. What else can you expect from losers like them?

July 2003

'Bore, bore, bore! That's what I am,' I told Janoo yesterday.

'I quite agree with you,' he replied with a smile. 'You are an awful bore.'

'*I* am not bore,' I said, 'life is bore. No visas to London and no visas to New York, no visas nowhere. All I can do is sit here and burn and die in this horrible clammy heat.'

'But you have a perfectly lovely cottage perched on a hilltop at the edge of a pine forest in Changla Galli,' he argued in that argumentative way of his. 'If only you could see it for the gorgeous place that it is.'

'Gorgeous, my foot!' I said. 'Why can't you be like everyone else and buy a mansion in Nathia instead of a hut in Changla? That way I could have met the same people that I meet every day for coffee, lunch and dinner in Lahore, and so nice it would have been.'

Janoo's only purpose in life, I think so, is to spoil my life.

Had he bothered to get me a place in Nathia, I could have gone roaring up the twisted hill roads in our Land Cruiser, exhaust blowing, music blaring and all the windows up to show that even in Nathia I can't live without air-con. I'd be sitting in the back with my Versace shades and silk sequence-encrusted tunic over tight jeans, diamond studs glinting in my years, hair blowing lightly in the breeze – sorry, forgot windows are up, so hairs can't blow – latest copy of *Vogue* lying open beside me, so everyone knows I'm reading-writing type, and Filipina maid in the dicky surrounded by Tumi suitcases – latest ones obviously – and Kitchen Cuisine cartons and massive bottles of Nestlay water. And on our backside, a small Suzuki following with our cook and sweeper. If I don't have my bathroom washed down every day I *tau* can't go. So sweeper is must.

But I'm damned if I'm creeping off to Changla with nobody to watch and nobody to make jay. Much rather stay puts. Janoo, of course, is threatening to go off with Kulchoo. Go a thousand times, I told him, for all I care. It's all his fault anyways that I'm stuck here for the whole of the summers. Anybody who had a little bit of get up and go has got up and gone to London. All you had to do, I told Janoo, is to suck up a little bit to somebody in the Brit visa office and beg a favour and we'd also be sitting in Royal China in

Baker Street where all the Sindhis and Karachiites go to have dimp sump, instead of which I'm stuck in Main Market, Lahore. How do you think everyone else has got visa? After all, Bunny's been, Sadia's been, Rabia's been, Amina's been – and Janoo says I can't go. Why? Because he says he refuses to gravel in front of the British for a visa. As if he was some Nawab's son who can't lower himself by gravelling like everyone else does. Donkey. Dog. Crack. Loser.

August 2003

Finally, we've made it to London. Sales-shales are all finished but I'd warned Janoo from before only that sales or no sales, Dior's saddlebag is must for me.

'A saddlebag? What's that?' he asked in that weary, half-ill voice of his.

'A handbag, what else?'

'What does it look like?'

'How should I know? All I know is that Sunny says everyone who's anyone's got it.' And that's reason enough to buy it.

So yesterday as soon as I got out of taxi and into flat and put my suitcases down, I went straight to Harrods. Poor things, Dodie and Diana were there in the window. Big-big portraits with lots of flowers. I missed them so much, so much, I can't even tell. Stood and said prayers for them. Then I wanted to do something in remembrance of Diana and suddenly I remembered how much she used to love shopping. So then I went in and shopped and shopped. Every time

122

I bought something I thought of her. Dior bag, her favourite make. Four pink Channel lipsticks, just like she used to wear. Versace dark glasses, like she wore to Versace's funeral. Goochy high heels, in size six like her. Six pairs. Just my little way of keeping her mammaries alive.

Bumped into Mehreen in the beauty hall, by the Estee Louder stand. Mehreen Moodi, who else? They're here to drop their kids off at college, *na*. Like Haroon and Sadia. And the Lakhanis also. Now that American visas are so hard to come by, people are turning to England universities. Even though they don't give any financial aids.

Sometimes I wonder whether Kulchoo should even go to college. He's become so strange, *na*. Last week he went on at me about some carnival in a place called Nodding Hill in London. I asked around and found to my horror that it's some kind of African demonstration. I had no intention of sending him, but Janoo as usual took his sides and said it was culturally expending and took him off.

So I also went off to do some cultural expension myself. I went to see *Bollywood Dreams*. *Hai*, so nice it was, I enjoyed so much, so much that don't even ask. I tell you, there's no musical arranger like A. R. Rahman, particularly now that he's become a Muslim. And honestly there's no place like London for making you feel as if you're back home. But a nicer home.

Next day Janoo asked if I wanted to come with him and Kulchoo to see some stuppid exhibition in a place called National Portraits Gallery and then something else at British Museum. But I thought, why do time waste? Instead I went with my friend Bunty to Royal China on Baker Street where Karishma Kapoor had lunch last week. She wasn't there but lots of Sindhis were there, flashing diamond nuggets and Channel glasses. So flashy they are. I had chicken corn soup, egg fried rice and prawn sweet-and-sour. Shouldn't say because it sounds ungrateful, but Dynasty in Lahore is better. Their food has more *masala*. And now that I've done everything that I'd come to do in London, I can go back. Right in time for Muddy Hashwani's wedding in Isloo and Dubai.

September 2003

I swear these poor peoples are so illitred. So ignorant. On top, they never even listen. Who? Oho, servants! Who else? For years I've told Aslam (the cook, for God's sake) till my voice has gone horse to stop having children one on top of the other. Did he listen? Never in a thousand years. Why should he? After all, I'm providing the servants' quarters, the food, the gas, electricity, water. And all the food from the kitchen that he steals also – a chicken and a milk carton here, a sack of rice and a bag of sugar there. And then Janoo pays for his children's school and for their books also. Aslam must be a millionaire by now. His whole celery goes straight into his pocket, all six thou of it.

He'd worked with The Old Bag, Janoo's mother, *na*, ever since he was a child. His father was their gardener. So when we got married he came to me in my trousseau. I tried to get rid of him many times, because he used to spy on me and report everything to The Old Bag and The Gruesome Twosome.

'Today they cooked this, costing that much, and tomorrow they are expecting so-and-so, and Begum Sahib waked at this time, and Sahib went out that time,' and on and on and on.

But Janoo wouldn't allow me to sack him.

He told me I thought Aslam was a fifth communist. 'Don't you?' he asked me.

'Who, me?' I asked innocently, wondering who the other four communists were.

Anyways, in ten years Aslam managed to have six children while Janoo and I only managed Kulchoo. Mummy and Aunty Pussy know all about these peoples. They say they think about 'That Thing Only' and that's why they have so many children. Not like us, who've got so many things on our mind and so many worries.

Now Aslam's second son, eight-year-old Billa, has gone and got lost, along with the cycle I'd provided for trips to the market. I mean, just look at them! They send the child out on *my* bicycle without even my permission, and at 7:30 p.m. so that it'd be dark and the guard couldn't see who was taking the cycle. And what for? To get a midwife from the market because Madam is too scared to tell me she's having a miscarriage. On the way, the kid fell into a ditch, damaged the cycle, searched his pockets and discovered he'd lost the five-hundred-rupee note advanced payment to the midwife. So he went crying to the fruit-seller at the entrance to the bazaar.

'How can I go home now?' he cried to the fruit-seller. Then he took the cycle and wondered off into the night. That much we learnt from the fruit-seller.

That was five days ago. Billa hasn't been seen since and neither has the cycle. Aslam and Madam are wailing all day long, the food's being cooked by the bearer or being sent for from Dynasty Chinese or Punjab Club. On top, Janoo's accusing me of insensitivity.

'It's all my fault, I suppose,' I said. 'I *tau* at least tried to put her on the pill. Did you ever try and get him to use condominiums? Or get his bits snipped off?'

PS – While I was writing this inside, there was a big fuss outside and it expired that Billa had been found. He'd gone to Janoo's mother's house and was skulking around there in her servants' quarters, too scared to come home and tell about the broken bike and the lost money. And look at her servants, so mean they are, they never even told! For five whole days they were hiding him and they didn't tell. When The Old Bag returned from Sharkpur today she found him there

128

and brought him over. Now she's sitting beaming in our drawing room as if she was some big detective like Hercule Parrot or something, and the boy's crept off to his mother, who has probably got another baby in her belly already. Honestly, I tell you, these peoples are also the limit!

October 2003

I just couldn't belief my years when Janoo asked if I wanted to go to the Latent Rehmatullah Ball in Isloo.

'Are you mad?' I shrieked. 'It's *the* social event of the year and you're asking if I want to go?' There are lots of upmarket charities in Pakistan *na* which are run by the rich from good baggrounds for the poors. Latent Rehmatullah does free eye operations for the poors and also throws very nice, very expensive balls every year in the winters.

For my outfit I called Shamael in Karachi and said, '*Hai*, please help, *na*. Please send me an appropriate outfit.'

So she said she'd send me a Suzy Wrong or somebody's outfit by Fed Ex. I wanted to tell to her that I don't want to wear secondhand but didn't because I thought that she's Karachi's top designer, and what if she minds. Now let's just hope this Suzy Wrong or whoever she is doesn't have BO.

Then Aunty Pussy begged me to take Jonkers along

to show him a girl or two. *Uff*, how bore, I thought, but at least we'll be able to go in her big Merc with gunman and all. Arrive in some style. Not like riding shamefacedly in Janoo's three-year-old Corolla. The ball was faaabulous, with red velvet tent, orchids, and me in my Wrong dress.

Only fly in the ornament was that we had to sit with Janoo's bore Oxbridge friends, who spent all evening exchanging long-long, bore-bore stories from their past times about university dawns (I think so they call teachers 'dawns' at Oxbridge) and college porters (they must be luggage carriers like our coolies at airports) and getting the Blues (or was it booze?) in cricket and rowing-showing. And then some loser, who was too poor to afford a car as a student even, started telling about how his cycle had got stolen one night from outside his college. So then I also started on a long story about how our cook pretended that the cycle we'd given him to do the groceries and all had got stolen while he'd been inside the butcher's shop in the bazaar but when I threatened to call the police, he quickly said that maybe the butcher would know and he went and promptly got the bike back.

'You should have threatened the porter or coolie or whatever he was called in your college with the police,'

I advised him. 'Always you will find that it's the servants who are at the bottoms of it. And anyways, just remember, the mention of the word police and they'll spill all the beens.'

They all stopped talking and stared. I suppose they hadn't been expecting such a clever respond. I just smiled serenely at all the losers, snapped my crutch bag open, took out my latest Channel lipstick, put it on, snapped my crutch bag shut and patted my Chop Suey outfit. They all suddenly started talking at the same time.

Aunty Pussy says people who go to Cambridge get overeducated and overexcited and become egg-centric. Apparently Oxford doesn't have the same effect. Because Janoo's never overexcited about anything. People who go to Oxford are called Oxen. Imran Khan also went to Oxford. That's the only thing Janoo has in common with Imran. They are both Oxens.

Everyone was there at the ball. Mouse and Zaheer. Salik Chundrigarh and Nadoo (from Hashim Raza family only), all the legally blonde girls, and Captain Farook, the captain of Latent Rehmatullah Ball Trust.

When Jonkers gave a charitable donation of half a million rupees, Janoo raised his glass to him and Jonkers beamed. I think so it was first time in six months anyone had taken notice of him. Janoo can

132

be nice like that. Sometimes. Thanks God Aunty Pussy wasn't there otherwise she would have snatched the money back and marched Jonkers back home. Poor thing, I don't think so he'll ever find a wife.

November 2003

I hate my friends. All of them. Every single lying, cheating, two-faced one of them. Why? Because they've stabbed me in the backside, that's why. While my innocent, trusting back has been turned on them, they've gone off and re-invented themselves, leaving me high and wry. And worst thing, on top they're making so much of money also.

Maha, who failed every year in the Convent and got three pink cards from Mother Andrews for being stuppid, has opened a school and made herself Principle, and even Faiza, whose house, Mashallah Mention, is on our backside, and whose every coming and going I thought I knew, has become a fashion designer! Quietly-quietly she's gone and installed three old hungry-naked-type tailors in her garage and now she's the owner of 'Faiza's Fab Fashion House'. This is the same Faiza whose mother still wears a *niqab*, and the same Faiza who, the first time she came to KC (oh for heaven's sake, Kinnaird College, what else?),

134

was dressed in a frock and a *shalwar*. Most worst Janoo's cousin, Nabila, who's never slept on anything but *charpais* (you know, the string beds that the poors in Pakistan use) has become a furniture designer and even opened a showroom. Just look at these traitors. What cheeks!

So I went straight away to Mummy and complained.

'I can't bear it,' I wept. 'If I hear one more time how successful they are and how popular they are and how much of money they are making I'll kill myself.'

Mummy narrowed her eyes into slips like she does when she's thinking hard and hissed, 'These silly little upstarters. We'll show them.'

'But *how*?' I wailed.

'Why don't you open an art gallery?' Mummy said slowly. Now you know why Mummy was head girl at Sacred Heart Convent. Because she's always been more clever than anyone else, that's why.

'All you have to do is to rent an empty room in a nice locality,' she said, 'and paint it white. Stick in some lights and put up a few picture hooks and there you are. Art Gallery! And you, Gallery Owner!'

But then we had to think of a name. I suggested Decent Art Gallery, but Mummy said no, it sounded too lower-middle-class.

'Bonanza?' I said.

'No, too upstartish.'

'Tasveer?'

'Too Urdu medium.'

'Marks & Spencer?'

'Isn't that already taken?'

So after many-many thoughts we finally hit on it. As soon as that was decided I rushed out to have my visiting cards printed. *Hai*, I'm so proud of them. They are light pink, like Rose Petal toilet tissue, and on them it says in curly purple writing: 'Art Attack (new art gallery), Gallery Owner and Arts Council: Mrs Butterfly Khan, expert in modern art and pictures and all.' I haven't got the gallery yet, or even the paintings, but first things first, no?

December 2003

So much of fun!! I'm *tau* going off my rocket with all the parties-sharties, weddings and dinners galore. And the polo! That's *tau* even more better. So many polo functions, and all by special invitation only so that no cheapsters could get in. Serves them right, I tell you. Trying to muscle in where they don't belong. Janoo's sisters, The Gruesome Twosome, kept calling, kept calling, begging for tickets. So shameless they are.

'*Hai*, Bhaijaan,' they pleaded with Janoo, 'please get tickets for us also.'

Janoo, being the push-over that he is, got them tickets in the VIP enclosure. I *tau* nearly blew a fused. Particularly after what they did to me last week only.

'Bhabi,' said Cobra, the Elder One, 'you must have seen the movie in which your Mummy is starring?'

'Which one?' I asked.

'*Haw*, don't you know? *The Mummy Returns*? All the time we were watching it we were thinking of you.'

So when the tickets arrived, I quietly removed them

from the dining table where Janoo had left them and had them sent to Mummy's with a note that said, 'I know you and Daddy already have two-two each but I thought you might like to take your maid and driver. After all, they are also human beings.'

When Janoo asked, I said, 'What tickets, baba? I *tau* never saw any except my own. Cross my heart and hope to die.'

Now let the ugly sisters take another swing at me and see what a tit for tit girl I am.

But what a pity that no glam Indians showed up at the polo. So much I was looking forward to entertaining Shahrukh Khan and Salman Khan and Hrithik Roshan in my new sun room with its pink wall-to-wall carpet and apple-green velvet curtains, sorry, drapes (these days only the aunties say curtains). Never mind, next time. But the Denim and Diamonds Ball was just too much, I tell you. All these trendy models and cute-cute polo players – don't want to sound biased but ours were the best. Indian Captain, Samir Suhag, was okay also but nowhere as cute as our Kublai Khan, who lost his teeth but not the match. Too bad they didn't come wearing their tight-tight jodhpurs and their sweaty shirts. So hot they look in them.

Now next in my diary is Sindh Club Ball, from where I'll rush back for Nazi and Mansha's son's wedding, and then back again to Karachi for the Marry Adelaide Ball, and then the Tapal wedding. I suppose I'll have to drag around the undead – Janoo who else? But as Mother Andrews at the Convent used to say, we all have our crosses to bare . . .

January 2004

Mummy's gone on Haj. And Aunty Pussy also. Daddy refused to go, said his summons hadn't come yet. And Uncle Kaukab *tau*, poor thing hasn't been same since he got beaten up by those thugs. So they've dragged poor old Jonkers along instead. They had to be accompanied by a male member, *na*, that's a rule. Otherwise you know what the Saudis are like.

'Cheer up,' I told Jonkers. 'Maybe you'll find a nice pious-type girl there. I mean after all, the whole world comes there. You're bound to get at least one simple, straight type in all those teaming millions.'

When I told The Old Bag that Mummy was off to Mecca on Haj she muttered something about cats and 900 mice or something. I *tau* ignored. Best is to ignore. That seclusion I've reached after so many years of marriage.

I told Mummy to do lots of prayers for me and mine, for my health, for my looks, for my social life, for my bank account. If I hadn't reminded her she was quite likely to hog God all to herself. Sad to say because she's my mother, but she's like that only. I also told her to bring me a litre of holy water from the holy land. It makes your skin glow, you know, it being holy water from the holy land and all. In fact, I even know someone – Mulloo's first cousin from her father's side – who was so ill, so ill, that doctors-shoctors, everyone had given up on him. Couldn't speak, couldn't eat, couldn't breathe even, but then someone told his parents they should send for holy water because only that could save him. So of course his parents imported a drum of it. The minute it arrived they started pouring it down his throat and you know what? By evening he was not just breathing again, he was eating, drinking, sitting up in bed, chatting, every-thing! As soon as he got out of hospital he immediately went off to Haj to give thanks.

That was three years ago. Now I think so he is living in a huge, big villa in Dubai, because he'd defaulted on some big-big loans from two or three national banks here and guvmunt is after him. But, apart from that small matter, by grace of God, he is in the pinks of health and he goes for Haj every year.

So what was I saying? Yes, what I want Mummy to bring for me from Saudi. Maybe some of those nice glass beads that everyone has on their coffee tables now and, if she got to Jeddah, then a string of Basra pearls. But please, no velveteen prayer rugs and those date packets. I have quite enough of those already, thank you. I told her she must be back in time for Basant. Can't wait for all those fab Basant parties.

February 2004

Mummy's come back from Haj without my holy water. She says she spilt it by mistake, but I don't belief her because she's come back looking ten years younger when everyone else who went in her group is at death's door. There was so much of infections there, *na*. Flu and fevers and meningitis and God knows what else. You know poors from all over the world come there bringing all their illnesses and infections. But it was a bit funny how God didn't make sure that nothing happened to the Hajis. Considering they'd come all that way for Him.

You should see poor Aunty Pussy – bride of Frankenstein, with big-big bags under her eyes and skin all lose-lose and pale type – well, as pale as anyone can be with Aunty Pussy's navy-blue complexion. So why should Mummy's face look all smooth and creamy, just like Jay-Lo's. If you ask me, she's guzzled all my holy water on the sly. It's all lies about spilling-shilling. She's swallowed the whole water cooler herself. She's trying to pull a fast one on me but I know she's drunk it. It's written on her face. And all this after doing Haj! Giving lies to your own children. Imagine! She's also brought me wooden prayer beads when I asked for Basra pearls. Well, that's the last time I lend her my waxing woman and my massage girl. Next time she can go to Cuckoo's beauty parlour near Main Market and stand in a line with all the secretaries and phone receptionists herself and see how that feels.

And look at that jerk Jonkers – he went all the way to Haj and he's come back single. What a loser! Couldn't even find one single girl in four millions Muslims.

I asked him and he said, 'Well, Apa, one million, really.'

I wish he wouldn't call me older sister. He's only three years younger than me and ever since he became bald he looks forty-five, which if I'm his Apa makes me . . .

'What do you mean one million, you crack?' I snapped. 'All the newspapers are saying there were four millions.'

'Well, about three quarters were men,' he said.

He also is so picky, *na*.

'And what about the other million?' I asked. 'Were they women or were they something else? Honestly, the older you are getting the more choosy you are becoming. You find fault in everyone. Now what was wrong with the remaining million women?' I asked.

'Of those, two thirds were over fifty, I'd say,' he replied scratching his shiny head. 'And of the remaining third, almost all were already married.'

'If you let small things like that stand in your way, you will never be able to find a wife,' I told him.

But I don't give a damn. He can remain single till the dhows come home. Life is busy enough with Basant and weddings and things to bother about my loser relatives. They can all jump into the canal for all I care . . . but it still hurts when your family stabs you in the backside, like mine have done to me.

March 2004

I think so it's been the most rocking week in Lahore's history. All the rich and glam Indians have been here for the cricket matches. Vijay Malya came. In his jet. Janoo says Vijay's got the alcohol business in India all wrapped up. Must be in packaging and gift-wrapping. But between you, me and the four walls, nobody wraps a present like Aunty Pussy.

Talking of which, poor Aunty Pussy and Mummy have been reliving all their pre-Partition mammaries. Aunty Pussy says Maharani Gayatri Devi of Jaipur was very beautiful (she's also come, *na*), and the famous English photographer Cecil Beating took a picture of her. I was sitting there in the lounge only when they were recalling their other mammaries, poor things, so old and all, *na*. They say Jinnah's wife was also very beautiful even though she wasn't a Muslim.

Jinnah's daughter also came. Lucky thing lives in Bombay with all the film stars. Dina Wadia, very extinguished-looking, all stately and dignified. I think

150

so she looks just like Mohammed Ali Jinnah, but in a sari. Saw her at Shahida Saigol's dinner only.

Hai, it was so nice to see all the rich-rich, glam-glam Indians. We would've got a complex if we didn't have celebrities of our own. Like Yusuf Salahuddin, who's Lama Iqbal's grandson. I told this glam Indian woman that he's Lama's grandson.

'What?' she said. 'All the way from Tibet?'

And I shrugged and said, 'Must be.'

By the way, I also want a private jet.

Only problem is we're loosing in cricket to the Indians. I asked Janoo, 'How many goals have they done?'

As usual, he got exasperated. Then he slowly explained all about cricket to me. I pretended to listen carefully, but honestly it was so bore I almost fell asleep. All I can remember is that you can play for five days non-stop and still have a draw. And there's a nightwatchman and a duck and some men play in slips.

All the rich Lahoris have been having parties for the Indians. Even the poors like rickshaw drivers have been giving them free rides and, listen to this, even Saleem Fabrics, which never gives you even one rupee off, has been giving them massive deductions. Honestly, such big hearts we have. But Mulloo says when we go to India it's not like that. A shopkeeper over there would rather die than give you a deduction. Their hearts are the size of a matchbox. And ours the size of Lahore Fort.

April 2004

Life is over. The Indians have gone back. The parties have ended. There is no more cricket and no more matches. There's nothing to do and nowhere to go.

But I'm so spired by our neighbours' big-big planes that I've decided to become Indian also. I'm going to wear saris, become a vegetarian and put that red stuff in my hair partition. I'm also chucking my Fear & Lovely cream because The Look is all dark-dark. My mission in life is to be just like all my new best friends across the boarder. I've even started speaking like them.

When people say to me why I have started doing all this, I reply, 'Because I am like that only.'

I told Janoo that I'm working on a complete transportation. 'Transformation, you mean,' he said patiently.

'Whatever,' I said softly, soothingly. I am a peacenik like Bapu. Oho, Gandhi, you know, Mohtrama. Like him I won't argue. I won't shout. Just do quiet, peaceful opposition.

I carry coconuts in my Prada bowling bag and smash

154

them against the entrance door of every house I visit. And I've stopped doing salaam. Instead I put my palms together and murmur, 'Hello-*ji*,' while doing that wobbly head thing.

Between you, me and the four walls, stiff cotton saris are a nuisance. All scratchy-scratchy and tight-tight. Kulchoo says I look like an Urdu-speaking ayah from Uttar Pradesh but I told him Gandhiji wouldn't like to hear him say hurtful things to his mother. I overheard Janoo and Kulchoo refer to me as 'Kasturba' (she was Gandhi's simpleton wife or something), but I pretended not to notice even though I wanted to scratch their eyes out. Instead I repeated to myself, 'Peace. *Ahimsa*. Gandhiji.'

Last night for dinner I'd ordered a thin, soupy-type *daal* with white rice and some peas. All vegetarian like they have in ashrams. Spoilt brat Kulchoo took one look at the block-print tablecloth spread on the floor and said, 'Whatever happened to the table and where's my cheeseburger and chips?'

'Forget burgers,' I said in my new, gentle *ahmisa* way. 'Forget chips. We are becoming homespun from now. This is your dinner. Eat, child, and grow strong.'

'But even the servants don't eat mush like this,' protested Kulchoo.

Then he asked Mohammed Hussain, the bearer,

what they'd cooked for themselves and the traitor said, 'Aloo gosht, Kulchoo Sahib.' So he had a big dish of piping hot *aloo gosht* brought to the carpet with fat, disgusting pieces of meat floating in with the chunks of potatoes.

I exclaimed, '*Hai Ram!* Chhee-chhee!'

I had to drink all the soupy *daal* myself, while sitting cross-legged on the floor. Because of Gandhiji I didn't want to waste anything. Next day of course I got the runs – and I don't mean cricket. That was my day of fasting for Janoo's life, like in my second fave film, *Devdas*. Of course the day dragged on and on with the fast, and by evening I was feeling so faint, so faint that I thought my soul had transmigrated already. First I cursed Janoo black and blue but in a gentle, quiet way under my breaths. Then I watched tapes of my fave Indian soap, *Kyunke Saas Bhi Kabhi Bahu Thi*, in which everybody looked like they'd got split skulls because of that red line in their hair. Gave me such a thumping headache.

Just as I was going to open my fast with a soupy *daal*, Janoo said, 'I presume you're going to burn yourself on my funeral pyre when I die.'

And then I remembered that film *Water* in which all the widows had their jewellery ripped off and their heads shaved and wore white cotton saris for the rest

156

of their long sad lives and I decided there and then not to be Indian. Which was such a relief, because then I could open my fast properly with *naan kebab* and *biryani* and chicken *tikka* sitting on my proper table on my comfy chair in my velour tracksuit. And yell and shout to my heart's content. *Hai*, it's so nice to be meat-eating, shouty Pakistani.

May 2004

Such a coo I've done, such a coo that not even General Musharraf could have pulled it off. Of course, Janoo's angels even don't know because he is so fed up with what he calls my 'puerile dementia with all things Indian'. Best is to leave him aside because he's like that only.

As my friend Faiza says, the latest accessory is not the Prada bag but an Indian slung over the shoulder. So when Didi and Sally and Minnoo can have rich-rich Indian friends, why can't I, hmm? I am also not me, if I don't hook a big, fat Indian fish. When it comes to these things, no one is a better hooker than me, that I can tell you from now only.

So I started my champagne to hook a rich Indian. I went to Mummy and Aunty Pussy and asked them who the richest Indians were. They know these things, *na*, because once upon a time they were Indian also. Before they were Partitioned. Anyways, Aunty Pussy told me that richest ones used to be the Maharajas and Nawabs and things, but now they're all poors and have put their palaces on rent and moved into little-little bungalows. The new rich ones, she says, all have names ending with 'ni'. They are Sindhi, but not like our Khuhros and Pagaros and Mirs and Pirs who have Land Cruisers and land only. These Indian Sindhis are Hindus. Natch. And biz types. They have private planes parked in Heathrow and swanky yaks moored off Can. Near Niece, baba. In the south of Spain.

'Families like the Lalvanis and Shivdhisanis and Ambanis,' Aunty Pussy said, 'understand?'

'Of course I understand, Aunty Pussy,' I snapped. 'I'm not crack, you know. You mean like the Thandapanis and the Jamdanis and Machhardanis, *na*?'

Aunty Pussy blew out of her nose like she does when her maid asks for a holiday. But I'd had enough, so I left with the 'ni' thing stuck in my head like Mummy's chignon pin.

Next day, while Janoo was hearing news on TV, it struck me. The minute Janoo left the house, I frantically called up Mouse in Isloo.

'Can you help me get an Iraqi visa?' I asked. (Mouse knows *everyone* in Isloo.)

'Sure,' she said, 'they're two a penny. But why do you want to go to Iraq now?'

'*Uff*,' I said, 'don't you know, the grandest Sindhi's there only?'

'What do you want with a Sindhi?' Mouse asked.

'Oh, just to be friends,' I replied airily. 'Is it a crime?'

'I suppose not. But what's a high-profile Sindhi doing in Iraq?'

'Not just high-profile, but grandest of the grand,' I smirked.

'Really? And who's that?'

'Grand Ayatollah Ali Al-Sistani.'

June 2004

Just got back from Karachi. So tired, *na*, but in such a good glowy way. Because I've had a hectic, beautiful weekend. Shahina and Shakil (Jang newspaper-*wallahs*), their son Ibrahim got married, to Khurshid and Zeba Hadi's daughter Sheena. One fab function after another. A monsoon flood of people. Everyone who was everyone was there. Even Janoo.

I said to him, 'Are you noting? This is the way to do things. When Kulchoo gets married I'm going to do same-to-same.'

I'm also going to invite everyone – except Janoo's family, of course. I can see them already, trundling in like a herd of dinosoars in their moth-eaten brocade saris and their big-big gold earrings and thick-thick gold bangles. Sooo last century. Sooo last millennium. Sooo not invited.

After returning to Lahore, I've gone to a few balls-shawls. That as Janoo says, is my meat and drink, *na*. One was for the charity, Care. And the other was not a ball but polo match. By Citizens' Foundry. They do education of poor children. Janoo says it's a very worthy project. He'd know. Being very worthy himself.

Talking of worthies, look at Imran. All those lectures about Brown Sahibs and how we should all take off our trousers and put on *shalwars* so everyone would know we were proud Pakistanis – rich coming from an international former playboy. And after those lectures about the importance of marriage then he goes off and gets a die-vorce. I'm not saying that he's not allowed to get a die-vorce, but please don't give so many lectures to everyone else. That's all.

I'm so disappointed *na* that don't even ask. I used to do so much of appraise of him when he was standing with Justice Party. And when Janoo used to tell me that a leopard never changes his sports, I used to tell him that you are just a bitter old bore and can't see any goods in anyone.

And that Jemima also. Sitting over here all hunched up with her head swathed in a *dupatta* like a shy bride and banging on and on about living in joint families and how much she loves wearing *kurtas* and *shalloos* because it's all about tradition and modesty and all.

And now she's bouncing around beaches and nightclubs with Who Grant, who isn't even her husband.

But one thing you can't take away from Imran, and that's his hospital. That *tau* is fantastic, even Janoo agrees. And one thing you can't take away from Jemima, and that's Who Grant. He *tau* is fantastic, even I agree.

Janoo's just too much. Last few months he's been talking about nothing except politics. Even at Salman Taseer's sixtieth the other day, he was going on and on about who's on the up and who's on the down. He was the only one on Jamali's side. Everyone else was on Musharraf's side. And nobody, but nobody, was on Bush's side. Bush *tau* got a lot of curses. I agreed completely. I told everyone how America is the route of all evil. Everybody hates America and Americans. It's the in thing these days. (Thanks God the American Council General wasn't there or visas might have become even more impossible.)

Janoo said, 'Somebody should be charged for what's happened in Abu Ghraib prison.'

I wanted to ask Janoo how much they should be charged. One million? (Dollars of course. Rupees *tau* even beggars in Main Market Lahore won't accept.)

164

Or five? Or ten, even? But then I got distracted by
the cake which came with sixty golden candles and I
started singing 'Happy Birthday Too Yoo . . .'

July 2004

Haw, just look at them. How mean they are, the terrorists, throwing bomb on poor Shock Aziz. Him being prime minister and all, what if he'd died? As I was telling Janoo, thanks God he was saved, poor thing, and no damage was done.

'What do you mean, "no damage"?' asked Janoo. 'Nine people died and you say no damage was done?'

'But, darling, I don't know those people,' I replied reasonably. 'How can you expect me to feel sorry for them?'

'You don't know Shaukat Aziz either,' persisted Janoo.

'But I feel I do. After all, we know so many of the same people. And I know his old home, City Bank, and I see him on TV. I didn't even know the names of the people who died.'

Janoo's not himself these days. I'm not meaning he's someone else, but just that he's not himself. He was always a bit of a kill-joy but these days *tau* his temper is so shortened, so shortened that you say even one small thing and he corrupts like a volcano. I think so it is the heat only. So many times I told him that let's go to London, but would he listen?

'I don't want to go to Blair's England,' he kept saying.

He may not want to go to Blair's England but has anyone asked me if I want The Old Bag to stay in my house? She's been sitting on my head now for the last three months while her house is being re-innovated. Why should she want her house re-innovated when she should be thinking of, you know, her next house, I mean the one upstairs, in the clouds? (I can't even say it straight because Janoo gets so upset.) After all, everyone has to go one day – even Musharraf – but the minute you put the words 'going' and 'The Old Bag' in one sentence, Janoo blows a fuse. Too over-sensitive he's become.

'How would you like it if I kept harping on about your mother's imminent death?' he asked me.

'My mother's death is not imminent because she is fifteen years younger than yours,' I replied. 'And she doesn't suffer from "sugar" and "heart" and "blood" like yours does. And nor is she always banging on about "when I am no more" and "after I leave" when she has no intention of leaving for anywhere, EVER!'

So then he got up quietly and went into the sitting room. I followed. Then he got up and went into the hallway. I followed. As he opened the front door and stepped out, I said, 'Going now, are you?'

He nodded wearily and shut the door in my face.

Haw! See how touchy he's become . . .

August 2004

The Old Bag is jumping on my nerves so much these days that don't even ask. She's gone and embarrassed me so much in front of my coffee party set that I've become the laughing stop for all of them.

This is what she did. I've told you, *na*, that my poor darling shweetoo Kulchoo got ill? Got bronckite-us. Bad cuff and high fever and all. First *tau* I made him do goggles with hot, salted water, but when that didn't make any difference I took him straight away to Doc Anwar. Anyways, he put him on antibionics and slowly-slowly Kulchoo started getting better. But of course The Old Bag doesn't trust me with her darling grandson's care, and after dropping a truck-load of hints about 'the right diet' and 'the right cure', she finally came out with it and insisted that we take him to see some crack faith healer of hers in Sharkpur where Janoo's family's lands and all are. But for once, Janoo took my side and told her that Kulchoo was in safe hands and he didn't belief in healers-shealers. Thanks God, I thought, that's the end of that.

Obviously not. A few days ago, I was having coffee party in my house – Mulloo, Sunny, Maha and her Toronto cousin Billie, who owns a whole building in My Ami, and my big coo, Anjali from Bombay, whose husband, Shekhar, went to school with Rahul Gandhi; they were all there. I'd got a fantastic blow-dry and was wearing my new shoes from the Prada boutique in Dubai. Anyways, there I was all glammed up and making chit-chat with everyone and laughing my tinkly laugh and being all socialist and sophisty and everything.

And then the bearer came stammering into the room after he'd just served the sandwiches, saying, 'Ji, B-b-b-egum Sahib, big B-b-b-egum Sahib . . .'

And I just knew there and then only that The Old Bag had arrived and I would live to regret this day. I just knew it, call it sick sense or whatever. And there she was, larger than life, in her Bata shoes with her 150-year-old handbag clamped in her armpit, barging into my sitting room with her driver in toe, who was dragging something on a rope. Imagine my horror when I saw it was a sheep! A real, live black sheep. Doing baa-baa in my sitting room in front of all my trendy friends, with all my Wedgewood china laid out so prettily and piled up with heaps of delicate sandwiches.

'I've brought it to take the evil eye off Kulchoo. Kulchoo must touch it,' The Old Bag announced. 'Call Kulchoo and then after he's touched it we will slaughter it on the driveaway.'

I was *tau* completely frozen outside and I had this silly little smile pasted on my face while inside I was boiling and squirming, sending thousand curses on her oiled head. Through gritted teeth I told her Kulchoo had gone for tuition.

'In that case, I'll wait,' she announced, and plonked her backside on my sofa beside Anjali.

And then to my utter, utter horror, I heard the sound of water running and I turned around and saw that the sheep was doing small bathroom on my antique Persian rug, and Sunny was howling like a hyena because her brand new suede Jimmy Choose sandals were being splashed, and then the driver pulled hard on the rope to take the sheep out and that stuppid beast backed into my coffee table, knocking my Wedgewood platter off it and upending a pile of egg mayo sandwiches on Mulloo's designer-clad lap, and she also started screaming and the driver began swearing and the sheep kept bleating and Anjali began tittering and over all the commotion I hear The Old Bag saying, 'Please to pass those chicken patties . . .'

September 2004

Nothing to report except that summers are going, thanks God, and if summers are going that means winters must be coming, but I expect you know that also. So, really, nothing to report.

October 2004

Recently I've been doing so much thinking, so much thinking that I feel as if I'm going to get a brain hemoroyd. I've been popping Lexxos (you know, my fave trankillizer, Lexotnils) to relax my nerves, but they've made not a jolt of difference. Must be fakes, or counterband as Janoo calls them. Half the things in Pakistan, from prime ministers to mineral water, they are fakes. As a result, all of last week I've spent in such mental turmoil that don't even ask. Now I know how poor old General Mush must have felt when Bush called him on 9/11 and asked him to choose between supporting America or supporting the Talibans. Decisions, decisions, decisions! But at least for him the writing was on the ball, for me there's no such luck.

It all started when I overheard Janoo's friend Habib – you know, Fida Ali, uppermost architect from Karachi only? – well, I heard him talking of something called 'minimalism' at a dinner party the other day. Apparently it's the 'in' look of interiors and gardens and all, in which even if you have enough to fill a whole museum you have to pretend that you are hungry-naked and have nothing. So your drawing and dining rooms should have only one or two decoration pieces. No glass-fronted cupboards stuffed full of heavy old silver tea services you got in your dowry, no piles of multicoloured paisley cushions, no big-big landescapes in big-big golden frames, no grand chandelayers, no cut-glass vases and bowls, no porcelain figurines, not even Ladro from Harrods. Curtains can't be swagged and fringed anymore. They all have to be linen and cotton, not velvet and brocade. Even your Bokhara rugs should be rolled up and put in the storeroom. (Now that mine has sheep urine stains on it, that's just as well.)

And if you still have all that ethnic painted furniture, then *tau* you are a total loser and should retire to Sharkpur where all the losers like Janoo's relatives live. But if you are hip and cool, then you should have a naked floor – but only if it's wood or limestones. Terazzo must be immediately uprooted. Prints are out. So no paisleys, and flowers *tau* are so over that don't even mention them. Weaves are in. And that too, in tired, dusty colours like moss, mouse, frog, mud. Flower buffets in crystal vases are out. Dry, thorny branches are in. Walls must be white. Furniture beige. And absolutely no carving-sharving. No curtains. Blinds only. Lamps have to be discreet and modern. Like me.

But what is giving me a brain hemoroyd is what to display now on the console table in my dining room? Should it be the big Gardener plate that I inherited from Mummy's aunt or the old silver tray? I keep thinking Gardener plate but it has flowers in the centre and flowers are *tau* totally out. Then again silver is also passay, but one tray I think so is okay. Habib says the trick to avoiding headaches, and I suppose also to look rich, is to circulate your stuff. Then *tau* I better put out the Gardener plate. At least it is circulate in shape.

November 2004

Janoo, I think so, needs to go on Prozac. Ever since
the beginning of November, he's been going from bad
to worst. First there was the American election. He's
taken Bush's victory so much to heart, so much to
heart that don't even ask. I think so he's more upset
than Senator Carry even. Just kept shaking his
unshaven face and muttering, 'How COULD they?
How could they vote Bush in?'

'Oh for God's sake,' I told him finally, 'what's to you?
He's their PM, not yours. Why are you eating our
heads over it?'

'Because what he does has ramifications for the
whole world,' he said. 'Look what he's done to Iraq,
what he's doing in Guantanamo Bay, what he plans to
do in Iran. And he's a president, not a prime minister.'

'Same difference!' I muttered to myself. I didn't tell
him that I was also disappointed. I was hoping so
much that Carry would win and then we'd get that
shweet young Edwards with his glossy hairs and Tom

Cruise smile as deputy PM or deputy president or whatever they call them. But instead we have to stare at that old bad-tempered bull, Chainy.

And then just as Janoo had begun to shave again, Yasser Arafat went into a comma. Again, Janoo became depress. Sat in front of TV all day, wouldn't go out, wouldn't see people. No parties, no dinners, not even any GTs for God's sake. I wanted to tell Janoo, it's all very sad and everything, but Arafat's not your paternal uncle, you know. But one look at his down-in-the-dumbs face and I thought better not say anything, otherwise he himself might go into a comma.

And then on top, America went and bombed Falluja. Lo, it was as if the Americans were bombing our own house. Janoo, if anything, went further down the hill. All day now he spends reading international news things on the Inner Net.

So I thought enough is enough, and I called up a brain doctor whose number Mummy gave me. Over the phone I told him that I thought my husband was going mad.

'Why?' he asked me.

'Because he's behaving so strangely,' I said. 'He's lost all his interest in life.'

'Please describe his symptoms.'

'Well,' I said, 'where do I start? He won't go to GTs.

And he won't take any interest at all in who I met at my coffee parties and what they wore and what they said. And he is least bothered about my best friend's husband's new car, which is bigger and more expensive than ours. And nor does he want to know who went on holiday where and how much of shopping they did and how big their bill was. He isn't interested in Bollywood, not even Shahrukh Khan. He didn't even want to know all the dirty details when I told him that one of our GT crowd, Sameer, had left his wife and run off with his telephone receptionist. Imagine! That's how ill he is. *And* if that wasn't enough, he spends all morning – at least two hours – reading newspapers and all evening reading books. And in his time off he watches TV and sighs and rolls his eyes when I switch the channel from BBC to Fox. I think so you need to give him Prozac.'

'I think', said the doctor, 'that I need to give him some sympathy.'

'Doctor,' I said, 'you are crack.' And I slammed the phone down.

December 2004

So many decisions I have to make these days. Like whether to have the floors pulled up and central heating put in. It gets so cold now, with winters lasting for at least one full month. And gas heaters are sooo last millennium.

And whether to tell Mulloo that her maid is having an affair with Faiza's driver. I know because my Filipina, Sandra, saw them. Or whether to wait till Mulloo's being more obnoxious than usual and then tell her.

And whether to have my eyebrows lifted and my neckline lowered.

And whether to send the cake that Psycho sent for Janoo day before yesterday to The Old Bag as a birthday present.

And what to wear at the *Good Times* magazine launch party for which Mira Nayyer is coming – you know, the one who made that film *Monsoon Marriage*?

I think so she's also made something called *Salaam Bombay* and *Vanity Fear* . . .

I tell you I have so much to think about that don't even ask. And then Janoo says I never think.

January 2005

I've got such bad *kismet*. The party season's on my head and I've gone and got bronckite-us. I've had such high fever that I swear I was like a gas heater. And I've had a bad cuff. And cold. And nothing's helped. The only thing that's helped is a homopath. Homopathics are very in these days, *na*. Nobody even looks at doctors anymore. And good thing also: any time you go to them, at once they put you on anti-bionics. I've taken so many antibionics I swear they've rotted my intesticles.

But despite of my illness, I've not missed a single party or wedding. Because I know how much people look forward to my coming. So first I went to Sheheryar Ali's wedding. Must say, it was a totally fit scene, with fountains and peacocks and jewels to die for. Nice plot they have for a party. Big-big, open-open. And the best address in Lahore: 1 FCC.

Then there was that lunch for Sara Sulehri. You know, the one who wrote that book *Meatless Ways*.

She teaches at Yales University. She's written a new book called *Boys Should Be Boys*. Lunch was nice but I left before the guest speaker's speech because I didn't want to miss the final episode of my fave Indian soap, *Kyunke Saas Bhi Kabhi Bahu Thi*.

But imagine what happened when I got home? Kulchoo was watching *The Meekest Link* on BBC. I told him to switch it off but he said first I had to buy him a Sony Flatron for his room. Look at him! When did he get so materialistic? Where does he learn it from? Must be school. Everything bad comes from there only.

Anyways. Then there was Ahmad Rashid's Christmas party, full of left-wings-*wallahs*, you know, Rashid Rehman, Najam Sethi, Ijaz-ul-Hasan, and the whole NGO crowd. Wearing handlooms and talking bore-bore things like politics and econmics. Food was good, but. Turkey and lamb roast and crispy salads with lovely dressing gowns.

After lunch I was feeling a little bit on the weak side, but then I took two of my homo pills and drove out to Bali's bash at his farmhouse in Bedian which is almost on the boarder with India. Everybody was there, including Shaukat and Marina who were visiting from New York. I hear Marina *tau* knows everybody who's everybody, including Coffee Annan, Woody Allen and Paris Hilton. I did lots of PR and rushed around saying hello to everyone – even those I didn't know, because I thought if they are at Bali's they must be important or rich or both. Preferably both.

February 2005

This bore tsumani is also not stopping. Now it's also come into our house. Taken off all our servants and all our clothes. It began with the new Bengali cook, Qamar-ul-Islam (didn't I tell you I finally managed to get rid off Aslam, The Old Bag's agent? He went back to her only). Qamar came and told me the wave carried off his entire village and that he must go back home just now only to find his family, all of which is missing.

'Six daughters, five sons-in-law, four sons, four daughters-in-law, twenty-five grandchildren and one wife, all missing?' I asked.

'Yes, Begumshobji,' he cried, dabbing at his eyes with his apron. 'All missing. House gone, family gone, cattle gone, life gone.'

First *tau* I felt like saying, 'And who's going to cook the big dinner I'm having for forty people next week?' But then I thought of Janoo sitting in front of the TV, shaking his head, and muttering, 'What a disaster!' At the time I'd thought he was talking about The Old

Bag, who is a walking-talking disaster, but later I realised he meant the tsumani. So I put a big stone on
my heart and said to Qamar that he could go but first
I must check with Sahib.

'No, Begumshobji, let me go just now,' he pleaded.
'I beg you.'

So, being the saint that I am, I retented, and on
top gave him twenty thou also to help rebuild his
house. He left grinning from year to year. It made me
feel so good, *na*, helping the needy like that. I swear
I felt the breeze of paradise fan my face.

When Janoo came home I told him of the big sacri-
fice I'd made. 'Qamar's gone,' I said.

'Where?'

'To East Pakistan.'

'You mean Bangladesh.'

'Whatever,' I replied airily.

'Why?'

'Because I think so we gave them freedom. And
they chose a new name.'

'Not Bangladesh,' said Janoo. 'Qamar. Why's he gone?'

'Because,' I said, speaking very slowly as if to a
retarded child, 'his village has been swept away by the
tsumani. And his whole family's missing.'

'But the tsunami never got to Bangladesh!' said
Janoo. 'For once Bangladesh was spared a flood.'

Haw, look at that fraud, Qamar. Let him come back and I'll fix him good and proper.

So when Sandra, my Filipina, came and said she wanted to take early holiday and go home to Vanilla, in Filipine, I blew a fuse.

'I suppose your family's missing also. Well, missing or not, no one is going from here till I say so.'

Then on top, at Kulchoo's school they've asked for donations for the tsumani victims. Can be anything – money, clothes, blankets, food, Kulchoo said. First *tau* I told him we'd already bought our sacrificial sheep and that's our donation to the poors done and delivered. But then he told me Sunny's son brought lots of clothes and tins of food, all packed by his mother in a neat brown parcel. Since Janoo is always doing complaints about my having too many clothes, I thought okay, let's get rid of all the ugly stuff I received at my wedding from The Old Bag. So I packed up a huge sack full of clothes: horrid old heavily worked satins and brocades and organza saris and, best of all, Janoo's grandfather's Nehru jacket that he wore on his wedding. It was made of burgundy velvet and was encrusted with old gold embroidery. When Kulchoo was small he had a wind-up toy monkey who played a drum. He wore an exact same coat and matching hat. Janoo's grandfather must also have been a bandmaster in his spare time. Honestly! On top I also sent the sacrificial sheep to the school. They can ship him off to Nepal, or wherever else the wave has reached.

But what to do about the lunch? I think so I'll just cancel it. Anyways, it was only Janoo's family. They can all do with skipping a meal. I'll tell them that I'm donating the money from the lunch to the tsumani survivors.

March 2005

Haw, look at our ex-chief minister, Shahbaz Sharif! Or actually, don't! You might not recognise him with his new hairs. I'd forgotten he'd had a hair transport until he announced his third marriage. I thought only young men – like in their twenties and all – who start going bald and can't nail good marriage proposals, get new hair. Not senior citizens. But then I suppose if you're marrying another senior citizen then you want to show, *na*, that there is still lots of life left in you.

But what I want to know is why Nawaz Sharif, elder brother and ex-PM, has also gone and got a rug on his head? He's not getting married again. Or is he? But you never know with men. Men can do anything anytime. That's what Mummy says. Not that poor old Daddy has ever done anything. He *tau* doesn't even dye his hair. But so nice he looks, *na*, so nice, with his grey hair to match his grey outlook. For that matter, even Janoo looks a bit like Richard Gear. But poor old Janoo has neither the body, nor the crinkly smile. Nor

194

the Pretty Woman, as that cow Mulloo added when I was telling her about Janoo and Richard.

Anyways, I must dash. Have to go to Isloo, *na*, to do condolence with General Musharraf for the death in his family (by the way, who exactly's died?). Lahore is wearing such deserted looks these days because everyone is in Isloo doing condolence.

Thanks God for the Lahore Book Fear. If it wasn't for the Indians who've come across the boarder, Lahore would have been totally lonely. Only pity is just the booky types have come. No film stars, no shrieking socialights, no business magnets. Just the quiet librarian types with cloth bags and grimy glasses. But never mind. Something is better than nothing.

April 2005

Summers are coming. Fans are on. In cars air-con is must. By the way, have you noticed how much of traffic there is on the roads suddenly? Yesterday it took me full hour to get home from Liberty Market. I'd gone to Saleem Fabrics to check out the new summer voiles but it would've been quicker to fly to Dubai and done my shopping there only. Janoo says it's because of all the car loans. The traffic, not the shopping. I know, I said. Every Tom, Dick and Hairy's got a car now. Even my waxing woman's son's got one.

Honestly, some of these new Suzuki-*wallahs* don't know how to drive even. Barging in from left, right and centre, taking up our parking spaces and behaving like real upstarters. Yesterday, when one stole my parking space outside Habib Bank just seconds before my driver was turning in there and I stuck my head out of the window and screamed at him, you know what he did? He said, 'This is a public parking lot, not your private garage!' And then slammed his car door and sauntered off, whistling with hands in trouser pockets.

Imagine! The cheeks! And you know what he looked like? Like one of those clerks, all thin and reedy, who used to quietly, uncomplainingly work for hours and hours in Daddy's outer office where there used to be only fans and no air-cons. And now they've got cars! And tongues! As Daddy says, 'Bhutto has a lot to answer for! He was the one who gave them damn-fool ideas about unions and talking back.'

Really, these people shouldn't be given loans and they shouldn't be allowed to drive! I'm saying for their own goods only. Tomorrow they'll bang up the car and who will pay the loan, *haan*? They will default imme- diately and it will be taxpaying, honest citizens like Janoo and me who'll be left with the bill. I said as much to Janoo and in respond he gave me a funny- type look. Let him give! I damn care. He's also such a two-faced hippo-crit, *na*.

Why? *Haw*, how you can ask? First when we won the cricket test match against India he said he was going to watch the one-day in Delhi. Then when we lost the one-days, in Coaching and that other place,

Vishakawhatever, he says what's the point? Of going to Delhi!

'Point?' I said, amazed at what I was hearing. 'Point? I'll tell you what's the point. Parties are the point. Seeing is the point. Being seen is the point. Coming on TV is the point. Making Mulloo envious is the point. Enjoying is the point. Shopping is the point.'

Then I told him what's NOT the point. Cricket is NOT the point. Bore thuk-thuk with bat is NOT the point. All those silly mid-offs and square legs and perverse swings and bore-bore things. They are NOT the point.

Well, if I'm not going to Delhi I'm going to Karachi for Habib Fida Ali's birthday party. It's his seventieth and very reclusive too. For 150 people only. All hand-picked, like the finest cotton. He's invited Sunny and she said she'd take me along. But what to give him? Crystal bowel? But I've heard he likes ethnic. Flopsy says he has miniatures and Gandhara and antique silk rugs and that sort of stuff. So shall I give brocade cushions? Very nice ones they are selling on backside of Ashraf Ali, Qamar Ali. With golden tassles. Or maybe camel-skin lamp. So much of headache. I think so I'll just buy him Versace dark glasses from Agha's only. If it's one thing you can never have enough of,

198

it's Versace dark glasses. And Goochy bags. And diamonds. And Prada. And Prados. And servants. And bank accounts. In sterling, but. Otherwise *tau*, you know how I'm always giving thanks to Allah for all He's given me and all.

May 2005

Janoo's just come back from a week in the mountains. Because he's re-innovating the cabin he's bought and apparently it's full of builders, he borrowed Mouse and Zaheer's cottage in Changla Galli (their friends call it 'The Mousetrap' because it cost a lot and took a long time to complete). Janoo said he wanted the peace of the hills. I told him I also want a piece of the hills, but I want a seven-bedroom mansion on it with servants' quarters and guest sweet and not a cute, quaint cottage. But who listens to me? Anyways, he came back very pleased with himself. I asked what he did do there and he said he went for long walks, watched DVDs and read by a log fire. Loser.

Went to a GT at Mulloo's last night. Dragged Janoo along just in case people think he's left me. You know how suspicious people are in this town. Always thinking the worst.

Of course, the minute we got in Mulloo asked me

in her shrill voice, '*Haw*, you didn't go to Changla? Why, but? There isn't some fight-shight between you two, is there?' she said, smiling like a fox who's just seen a fat, defenceless hen.

'Not at all,' I replied airily. 'It's just that it's simply too bore for me. Take away the mountains, the forests, the waterfalls and the views and what's it got? Nothing!'

And then Janoo, bore that he is, started banging on and on about the joys of Changla and how lovely it is to spend time commuting with nature. So of course Tony – he is so competitive, *na*, that he'd strangle his own twin in his mother's womb if he could – he also started on about all the nature he saw on his last trip abroad. And how it was nicer than the nature that Janoo saw. Cheapster.

'But didn't you go to Bangcock then?' asked Janoo, puzzled.

'Yes, but there also you see the sky and breathe the air. Allah's creation is everywhere.'

'But you know,' said Mulloo, in her most tired-type voice. 'We *tau* have travelled so much, so much that every place has become bore. Now last year Tony dragged me off to Venice. I'd heard so much about it, that there's no place on earth like it and that it's totally unique and when we got there, guess what we found? It was all flooded. Couldn't even step out of the hotel room without falling into a river. And that also all brown-brown, dirty water. Probably bubbling with cholera. From there we went to Rome and it was all broken-broken. Worse even than Mohenjodaro. That Collerseum of theirs, it needs more work doing than Maha's face. Thanks God there were some nice shoe and bag shops in Rome, otherwise *tau* it would have had nothing. Also there was that nice jewellery shop, Burglary, where I managed to spend a few hours. And then someone suggested we go and see, what's that place, Tony? In Spain, that we went to? Yes, Granada, to see that palace. What's it called, that palace?'

'Buckingham?' I suggested.

'No, not Buckingham.'

'White House?'

'No, no. It's named after that general store in Main Market. That one between Pioneer food store and that boutique. What's it called? Alhamra! Yes. I knew it. See? Alhamra Castle. I'm not saying it wasn't nice. Of course all those Islamic buildings and everything are very pretty in their place, but really not so much different to the Lahore Fort, no? I mean, why go all that way if you're just going to be greeted by the Fort at the end of it? And *uff*, so crowded, so crowded, even worse than Oxford Street in July sales. I said to Tony, I said, I *tau* am not used to all this pushing and shoving. Take me from here now only to my own peaceful little seven-bed house in Gulberg. Really, east or west, home is best. No, Tony?'

'Absolutely,' said Tony. 'Home, and Patpong.'

June 2005

Janoo and I are not on talking turns. We've fought *na*. Again.

It all started with a teeny-tiny request from me. You know how down to hearth I am, how I crave the peaceful, simple life, deep in my hearts of hearts. So into fresh air I am, so much a lover of green lawns and big-big trees and long-long driveaways and huge-huge farmhouses – no, no, I mean cosy little farm-houses. So I said to Janoo as we were driving back last weekend from one of our friends' farms in Bedian how nice it would be to have a tiny simple cottage there also, to which we could invite all our smart friends from Lahore and have open house and casual GTs with barbecues and born-fires. I said only this much and he blew a fuse.

'In case it's escaped your notice,' he said, 'you are the mistress of a sprawling great farm in Sharkpur that you have not deigned to visit for four years, and since you mention a tiny simple farmhouse, my ancestral home—'

'Oh, that pile of 300-year-old rubble!' I pooh-poohed. 'Only a loser would want to go to that Godfor-taken house, which doesn't have a home cinema or a gym even.'

'It's an authentic eighteenth-century *haveli*, not an ostentatious nouveau mansion with Doric columns and a Palladian façade masquerading as a farmhouse.'

'You're just jay because nobody likes your stuppid old Sharkpur or your bore family or your crum-bling old house, while everyone just adores Bedian,' I replied.

Anyways, there was a bit of argument and now Janoo and me are not talking.

But imagine the knives that stabbed my heart when I saw Liz Hurling in Bedian (she looked so nice in that white sari with sequence) accompanied by that Arun Nayyer with his dreamy smile. If I'd had a farmhouse in Bedian, I too could have invited her and been a dignified, salacious hostess. And tomorrow when Kulchoo got married we could have had at least three of his seven wedding functions there only.

But none of my dreams are ever going to come true, and you know why? Because I'm married to a kill-joy, bore loser called Janoo – that's why!

July 2005

Look at these spoil-spots, these bombers! Going and
blowing up the tubes in London. And almost all of
them Pakistanis. Honestly! So mean of them, so
selfish. The least they could have done was to think
of us, sitting here boiling in the heat of Lahore.
Already it was so difficult after 9/11 for us to get
visas to London and New York; now *tau* it will become
impossible. Visa officers will beat us with their shoes
when we ask.

I'm not saying the bombers shouldn't be allowed to
kill themselves. It's a free world after all. So if they
want to, they should be our guests, or rather, Allah's
guests. No one's stopping them. But they should have
the decency to go hang themselves from a tree or jump
off a tall building or into a well or whatever. Why take
along computers, I mean commuters, who don't want
to go, whom you haven't asked even? Maybe they don't
want to go to paradise just yet, no?

I asked Janoo. I said, 'Since you're Mr Know-All,

please tell this to me: why are these suicide types such spoil-spots?'

He muttered something about cultural alienation and econmic delusion and political powerlessness and other bore-bore, stuppid-stuppid things like that, but when he saw me yawning he said, 'It's like this: they feel that nobody cares about what they think and so they feel ignored and angry. And this is one way of making themselves heard.'

'With a bomb? You mean make such a loud explosion that everyone goes deaf? That way you're going to make people hear the things you want to say?'

And then the more I thought about it, the stranger it seemed to me. I mean like if Mulloo didn't invite me to her parties and didn't care about how angry and ignored I felt, would it make sense for me to arrive uninvited to her next do, push myself in with all her guests and then blow myself up in her sitting room? No, because not only would I not be invited to any more parties – because I'd be dead and dead people don't get invited anywhere – but poor old Kulchoo's social life would also die. Janoo would be unaffected because he *tau* never had a social life in the first place, but Kulchoo and I would be toast, as they say in Hollywood. I would be toast in more ways than one, but who knows, Mummy might find herself exuded from her bridge group, and even Aunty Pussy might find herself a person *non granta*.

And Jonkers *tau* can forget finding another wife ever. They will say, '*Haw*, don't you know, he comes from *that* family, only. The one with suicide bomber. No, stay away from them. Too dangerous.'

And also, as I pointed out to Janoo, if I kill the same people that I want to be invited by, then who's left to invite me, hmm?

For once he agreed with me. 'Well, yes,' he said. 'You do have a point.'

Honestly, it's so simple and straightforward. If only the bombers had consulted me before, none of this would have happened and we would all have been fine with visas in pockets and Pakistan's reputation in tact. I think so I should set myself up as consultant. Bomb consultant and explosives expert. How does that sound? Good, no? Maybe I should put that in the bit where it says 'profession' in the passport. I think so it would impress the hell out of visa officers.

August 2005

He's left me! Imagine, after all these years, after all I've done for him, he's gone without even a backwards glance. Who knew his name, even? Tell? I brought him out, I made him famous. And this is how he replays me. Mummy was right: never trust a man. He'll always double-cross you in the end. Leave you hanging high and fly. Men are made like this only. He's gone to Dubai. Thinks he's going to make it big there. Who does he think he is? Some Russian senorita with golden hairs and blue-blue eyes?

Once my Iraqi dinars make me rich, my shoe won't even care. I've bought so many-many, and that too dirt cheap, that when Iraq is back on its feet and Iraqi dinars become more expensive than dollars then I'll be the world's richest person. I'll also become a famous oil magnet like Bill Gates. I called Mummy and poured out my brain to her. Didn't take very long. But just look at Mummy – she's become so selfish. Any other mother would have been so heart-warning but she didn't even give me an ounce of sympathy.

'Don't you think you're overreacting to his departure?' she said. 'After all, he was only your tailor.'

'*Tailor?*' I screeched. '*Tailor?* Master Bashir wasn't just a tailor. He was my *shrimp*. I used to tell him everything and he used to advise. You know how he used to bring his sowing machine and come and sit in the house and watch all the comings and goings with his beady little eyes and then advise me on how to put The Old Bag and The Gruesome Twosome in their places. And he was my spy. He used to tell me exactly what fabric Mulloo and Sunny and Baby and all had bought and how they were planning to get it stitched up – he also had his spies among their tailors, *na* – and so before they could have a chance to show off their new outfits, I'd already had them made exact same to same, worn them and cast them aside. Also, who will sow my sari blouses in the Kajol-style now?'

'I know, I know,' she soothed, 'but I still think you're overreac—'

'Over? Me? Over? What do you think you are in your maroon platforms and maroon nails and maroon hair? Over! That's what. So, so over!'

Silence. And then Mummy said in a tight little voice,

'I think after this little outburst you and I are also over.' Click. She'd hung up.

After her menoapplause Mummy's also become so sensitive. Say one little thing and she flies off the candle. Now I suppose I'll have to go round to hers with a Channel No. 5 bottle and make-up with her. And then I'll have to steal Master Ramzan from my friend Farnaz. So many risks I'll have to take, so under-hand I'll have to be and so much of expense I'll have to go through to allure him away without Farnaz finding out it was me who did it. Janoo will hit the ceiling. Better call Mulloo first and find out if they've found oil in Iraq yet.

September 2005

You know, *na*, that I've always thought Jonkers was a bit of a loser. Now look, Mummy has me – sophisty, smart, connected – and poor Aunty Pussy has Jonkers – shy, shabby, disconnected. I mean, is there any comparison? But then this thief thing happened and he went up a hundred-hundred times in my steam. So much of pride he has, so much of honour. I tell you, he's become the protector of our family's good name.

It happened like this: Aunty Pussy and Uncle Kaukab had gone to Peshawar for some death in their extended family last week. Jonkers' paternalistic family is from there, *na*. So Jonkers was all alone at home. Anyways, the servants had given him dinner and skunk off to their quarters. As you know, all the time servants are running off at the smallest excuse to watch TV in their quarters. I tell you, their celeries should be halved. Anyways, Jonkers hadn't got anywhere to go, even though it was Saturday night, so he'd gone to sleep. Poor thing, he's such a social failure. Not like us who have to refuse 20-20 invites every night.

In the middle of the night, he felt someone pushing him roughly. At first *tau* he just mumbled and rolled over because he's used to being pushed around, but when he felt something hard pressed against his forehead, he woke up with a jolt. He reached for his glasses and put them on and discovered that there were four robbers in his room. One of them had put a devolver to Jonkers' forehead and was demanding that he open his safe. And he was not using very nice language also. No 'please', no 'kindly', no nothing. At first Jonkers nearly fainted with fright but when they grabbed him by the collar of his pajama jacket and marched him to the safe, Jonkers, poor thing, compiled.

Thanks God, Aunty Pussy is a miser who never, ever airs her jewellery (or whatever's left of it, after Miss Shumaila ran off with all that stuff), so that was all fine in her bank locker. When Jonkers finally managed to open the safe with trembling fingers and a gun plodding him in the back, he found a single brown envelope sitting there. The robbers snatched it from his hand and ripped it open and discovered only a pathetic 5,000 rupees in it!

'Only five thou?' smeared the robbers. 'And you call yourself a wealthy businessman?'

Now, so far all of this rudeness Jonkers had taken in his usual quiet, polite way. But now *tau* his blood boiled. This was too much. Imagine! Questioning his bagground.

'How dare you?' he shouted. 'Take me to your car at once!' (He would have used *his* car, but Aunty Pussy had gone in it to Peshawar.) Dressed in his striped pajamas and slippers, he took a ride on the back of the robbers' motorcycle because, cheapsters, they didn't have a car even and took them straight to an ATM. There he took out all the money he had in it (I think so it was at least 50,000). He slapped the crispy notes in the hand of the chief robber and shouted, 'Here! A present from a wealthy businessman!'

That's why I respect him from the bottoms of my heart.

October 2005

I'm firing Shanaz, my new maid. She's cut my nose and blackened my face. Thanks to her, I will never be able to hold my head up high in front of Mulloo or anyone else again.

Mulloo called up yesterday after lunch. Shanaz picked up the phone and when Mulloo asked, 'Where's Begum Sahib?' she replied, 'Sitting on the toilet.'

Imagine!! I heard her with my own years from the bathroom. I *tau* nearly had a heart attack. Honestly, these people are so crude! So I charged out of the bathroom like a heat-seeking missile and, grabbing her by the wrist, hissed, 'How many times I've told you that if someone calls and I'm in the bathroom you are to say that I'm taking a shower?'

'But you weren't taking a shower, you were peeing, I could hear it through the door!' she whined.

'I wasn't peeing, you understand?' I screamed. 'I never pee or do anything else on the pot. I NEVER sit on the pot. I only ever take a shower or wash my

220

hands. Yes, you can say I'm washing myself for prayers if Sahib's mother calls. But I'm never peeing. Never, ever!!' And then I sacked her.

Haw, look at this earthquake. So bad, no? Seventy thousand people dead and God knows how many millions injured. We were watching it on TV last night, all those lines of people huddled outside in the snow besides their wrecked homes, when Kulchoo came into the room and gave Janoo an envelope.

'What's this?' asked Janoo.

'My pocket money and all the birthday money that I've saved. I want you to send it to the people who've been affected by the earthquake.'

So Janoo hugged him and promised to send it right away. And then he said that he would hire a truck and fill it up with medicines and blankets and food and water and powdered milk, and he'd take it up to the mountains himself.

So Kulchoo looked at me and said, 'And you, Mummy, what will you do?'

'Me? I'll call up Mulloo, Sunny, Baby and all and tell them how much we've given.'

November 2005

All day, all night, Janoo rants about bore-bore things like Talibans and Al Qaedas and jihadis and wahabis and suicide bombers and ISI and God knows what-what else. He says fundos are everywhere and while Gulberg and Defence-*wallahs* are attending fashion shows and planning weddings, they are quietly organising the biggest GT ever, which, whether we like it or not, the whole country will have to attend.

'You watch!' he says. 'You just watch!'

At first I ignored, but after a while he got so much on my nerves with his damn-fool *fatwas* that I also exploded. '*Uff Allah*,' I said, 'if I hear Al Qaeda-Shaeda one more time, I'll scream.'

'You're already screaming,' he said quietly.

'So where are your Talibans? Under this table? Where are your bombers? Behind this sofa? ISI in the cupboard? For God's sake, they are in Waziristan, a thousand miles away. No one is in Lahore. Gulberg is safe, safe, safe. Okay?'

222

I called Mummy and she said someone must have done black magic on him and I must immediately slaughter a sheep and have the Quran read loudly to chase away evil spirits. So I sent the driver to the local mosque where the *mullah* wears a green turban with a long tail, and paid him to do a Quran reading in our names. Obviously I didn't tell Janoo, and nor did I tell him that I'd given The Old Bag some dosh also to kill a sheep in Sharkpur in his name. You know what he's like, *na*. Communist.

Anyways, to cheer myself up after that I organised a Holloween party. After all, I'm also human being, no? Got a party organiser – sweet-type girl who Maha knows – to do up house. She went and draped it with cobwebs and stuck big hairy spiders who look just like The Old Bag and splashes of fake blood on the walls and arranged brooms and fake bats and melting candles here and there. I made the servants dress in black with ashes put in their hair. I also told guests they must dress scary-scary. Mulloo asked what she should wear and I told her to come as she was, because she looked like a witch anyways. I don't think so she's coming anymore. God knows why.

Party was to be at 11 – and at 8 the bell rings and who should walk in but The Old Bag. Straight from Sharkpur to tell me about the sheep. Bearer opened the door in his slashed black clothes, bloodied face and ashy hair. The Old Bag took one look at him and then behind him at the blood-splashed walls and cobwebs and dark-dark lightning and she screamed, '*Ya Allah!*' And she whipped out her little Quran from her bag and started reciting from it and blowing and backing away from the door. Kulchoo came just then, but he was also dressed as a skeleton and when she saw him she *tau* passed out. So I had her sent home like that only. It took four men to lift her and put her in the car and I had a *lovely* Holloween party.

December 2005

There's to be a dinner at our house. Big and bore. With whole of Janoo's family. The Old Bag is coming with her 1,000-year-old maid; The Gruesome Twosome are coming – that's Cobra, her loser husband and children, and Psycho with her crack husband and tribe of children and a thousand bore-bore, ugly-ugly rellies whose names I now forget. Why? Because Janoo's the son and the head of the family and it's his duty to gather all the members of his loser family under his roof at least once a year. That's why. Otherwise *tau* when it comes to arranging marriages and standing for elections, nobody bothers to give him a second's importance, but when it comes to splashing out and doing big-big expensive things, he immediately becomes head of family.

Now look at Psycho, she's gone and got her daughter engaged to this very unsophisty but very rich family from Faisalabad – you know, the kinds who have fridges in the dining room and cases of mangoes under their beds? Well, apparently the proposal was made ages ago and the gold bangles were also put on last year on her fat wrists, but they told us only when the engagement cards were being printed and pretended that everything has been done just now only. And look at The Old Bag, such a snake in grass she's turned out to be. She kept it from her own son since she knew that Janoo would object because he has soft spots for Nicky – or Nikki, as her name is – you know, 'small' in Punjabi – who he thinks should study more and become something. Well she *is* going to become something, I told Janoo – a big, fat, unsophisty Begum with fat gold bangles on her wrists and a case of mangoes under her bed!

Well, Psycho was dropping hints left, right and centre that Janoo should have a big family dinner in his house and also invite Nikki's in-laws. And I bet they will want Janoo to shower gifts on boy and girl. And who do you think will pay for the gifts? Janoo, of course. Snatch crusts of bread from his own poor Kulchoo's mouth in order to feed cream and honey to nasty Nikki and her nouveau husband. Over my dead buddy.

But one thing Mummy and Aunty Pussy have taught me. Never do open fighting. Instead do clever, hidden fighting, like a gorilla. So this is what I did: I got

Mulloo, who was going to Bangcock, to buy me two watches – fake gold Rolexes from the Sunday market but in nice-nice, real-looking boxes, for ten dollars each. I told her they were for the servants.

Anyways, when she brought them, I showed them to Janoo and said, 'Look, I got these from Dubai on our last trip – from money I'd saved from household expanses. Nikki and her husband are going to come to our house for first time. We should give them something nice, no?'

'Aren't these a bit much, though?' Janoo asked. 'I was thinking of giving them just twenty thou each.'

'Oh, no, no,' I laughed. 'What is twenty thou these days? Can't even have a decent meal with that. If we are giving, we should give nicely. After all you ARE the head of the family . . .'

January 2006

I was supposed to go to Karachi for the Marry Adelaide Ball for New Year. It happens every year at New Year. And I want to go every year but Janoo never wants to go, so I have no choice except to stay at home and eat Janoo's head for not taking me and then drag him around to at least fifteen parties in revenge.

But this time Baby and Sunny said, 'We know how much you want to go to Karachi and we also know how going alone looks desperate in a woman of your age, so you come with us. You can sit at our table.'

What do they mean, 'woman of your age'? Sunny may have been one year behind me at school but only because she failed three years. And each year she failed and was kept back, her age also got one year less. Had she stayed at the Convent of Jesus and Mary and continued failing every year, she would have been the only sixteen-year-old in nursery. But her luck changed when she failed for the fourth time. Her father was posted to Pindi and she went off there to

Presentation Convent pretending to be seven when she was actually ten.

So first I wanted to tell Sunny to go to hell, but then the thought of the ball made me swallow my pride. After all, big things need big sacrifices. I mean, when Nehru offered Jinnah Pakistan without Kashmir, Jinnah also took, no? When I got home and asked Janoo, he said it was a splendid idea, the best suggestion he'd heard all year, and that I must go. In fact, he insisted I stay in Karachi for as long as I wanted.

'You mustn't rush back,' he said. 'Stay until Feb, March, if you like.'

'*Haw*, but won't you miss me?' I asked him.

'What? Miss you? Of course, of course. But we'll manage, Kulchoo and I. It will be hard, but somehow or the other we'll find the strength to cope. Isn't that right, K?'

And Kulchoo, shweetoo, who was drinking a milkshake – I think so it was vanilla – nearly choked.

So immediately I said, 'No, no, I'll stay if it makes you upset.'

But Kulchoo, who was now cuffing and spluttering, shook his head a thousand times and the minute he got his voice back he said over and over again, 'No, no, please, you mustn't stay. Abba's right. Go, stay for a month, two, three months.'

Everything was ready. Table had been bought, air tickets booked, designer outfit ironed, hair ironed, face ironed, I mean facial done – and then like a fool I decided at the last minute to go and consult Mummy's sooth-slayer. Mummy has one she's been going to in Model Town for years. She checks with her even before she goes to the bazaar. Her name is Baji Firdaus and she's never, ever wrong. She once told Mummy to be aware of black. And that day, very same day, as Mummy was going to a big lunch at the Punjab Club she stubbed her toe on the side of her bed and it turned all black. Baji Firdaus even predicated Twin Towers. Imagine!

So anyways, you know, *na*, that I've never been a very good flyer in planes, so despite of myself I asked. And you know what she said? 'What goes up must come down.' Or something like that.

Immediately I knew what she was talking about. So of course I didn't go. Only a fool would travel after such a clear warning of a crash. Janoo was very puzzled and sorry also. Kept asking why I'd changed my mind and tried to get me to think again. Even offered to go drop me himself in Karachi. Of course I didn't tell him why I wasn't going because he'd have laughed till he cried. He doesn't belief in sooth-slayers, *na*. Because he's a septic. But I kept saying, 'Didn't feel up to it.'

And Kulchoo, my little baby, *tau* looked actually so disappointed, so disappointed that don't even ask. So much he wanted his mother to have nice time. See, so much my family cares for me . . .

February 2006

Janoo and me always have this thug of war over Eid. He says we have to go and have Eid lunch with The Old Bag, and I insist that we should have it with Mummy and all. It's always a tossed up and the casting vote goes to Kulchoo.

'That's not fair!' I protest every year to Janoo, 'you know how mercury Kulchoo is.'

'Mercenary. The word's "mercenary".'

'Kulchoo'll opt for the place he gets the best Eidi presents and you know how The Ol— Ammi spoils him with envelopes stuffed full of money. Not like Mummy, who's strick because she knows the value of a good brought-up.'

So it's always lunch at The Old Bag's and dinner, if we're lucky, at Mummy's. Kulchoo makes a fortune and I have to dish out to The Gruesome Twosome's nasty kids and all The Old Bag's servants and God knows who else. I tell you, Eid's no fun if you're at the giving end. I'd much rather just continue with

234

Ramzan – feast at dawn, say your prayers and then sleep till it's time to open fast with big feast at sunset. So simple, so holy, so unfussy, so inexpensive.

Anyways, we arrived there and found The Gruesome Twosome and their tribe of brats dressed in ugly horrible *shalwar kameezes* made of durex or lurex or whatever it is. All I know is that their clothes were very ugly and despite of being brand new, very last year. But you know me, *na*, always so polite, so dignified. So I didn't comment. Just gave The Gruesome Twosome one long look from head to toe and then, with a smallish smile, went and sat in a corner and started sending text messages to Mulloo, Mummy and all, saying Happy Eid to everyone. But I swear Janoo's family can't leave me in peace for one minute even.

First maid came with juice. 'Please have,' she said. 'What juice is it?' I asked.

'Pomergranate,' she said.

'I hate pomergranate,' I said, jabbing the keys on my phone.

Then another maid came with a plate of something greasy and shoves it under my nose. 'Have *samosas*,' she said.

'I'm doing Atkins,' I told her, pushing the disgusting plate away.

Then the brats came and stood in front of me. 'Happy Eid, Maami,' they said, looking pointedly at my bag. Such greedies, I tell you. Honestly! So I opened my bag, opened my wallet and gave them a 100 each. They looked at me with dismay. Janoo had given me 1,000-rupee notes for children's Eidi, but I kept those well hidden in the inside zipped-up department of my bag. They're for other more deserving people, like Maha's nieces, whose parents have a huge flat in London Knightsbridge where I will *inshallah* go and spend whole of summers next summers.

Then lunchtime came. Usual bore unsophisty food: *aloo gosht*, *nargisi koftas*, *biryani*, *chicken qorma*, *chicken karahi*, *behari kebabs*, *shaami kebabs*, *seekh kebabs*, *pasandas*, *saag gosht*, *tawa fish*, *shabdeg*, *haleem*, *brain masala*, *keemay-waalay naan* and *siri payas*, followed by *shahi tukras*, *kheer*, *badaam ka halwa* and some cake from somewhere. The Old Bag's cook also knows nothing.

Anyways, they kept insisting I eat, so I looked at the table and said, 'But what *is* there?'

Just then, thanks God my phone rang. It was Mummy.

'Yes, Mummy,' I said, sitting at the lunch table sandwiched between The Gruesome Twosome. 'I'm coming. As soon as I'm done from here. They're serving lunch so it won't be long now, hopefully. Yes, and please wait lunch for me. You know I can't take greasy food.'

On the way home Janoo wouldn't talk to me. He said I'd been rude and ungrateful. *I'm* ungrateful? What about him, who never even thanked me for wasting half my afternoon on his precious rellies? Honestly, I *tau* have seen with my own eyes now. The more you do, the more taken for granted you get. Only good thing was, Kulchoo got given 10,000 Eidi. Thanks God, at least someone is happy.

March 2006

Such a huge big fight Mummy and Aunty Pussy have had. It was over Jonkers. At least I think so it was over Jonkers, but maybe it was about more. Maybe it was about them, the two of them. But outshot is that they aren't speaking and I don't think so they are ever going to speak. To each other, that is.

It all started when Aunty Pussy complained to Mummy that I wasn't flapping enough hands and feet to help Jonkers find a new wife.

'All she cares about are her coffee parties and her lunches and her hairdresser and her tailor,' grumbled Aunty Pussy. 'So selfish she is, never thinks about introducing my poor old son to anyone worthwhile.'

'But only last week she took you to meet that girl,' said Mummy.

'Which girl?'

'The teacher, Pussy. You know, that girl with the teeth.'

'*Girl?* You call that buck-toothed, grey-haired, elderly

238

person a *girl*?' shrieked Aunty Pussy. 'If those are the sorts of girls she is going to show Jonkers, she might as well not bother. I mean, *really*!'

'She wasn't grey-haired,' protested Mummy. 'She had golden streaks.'

'Everyone knows girls put in golden streaks when they want to hide the silver streaks.'

'What do you mean?' demanded Mummy. 'My daughter has gold streaks.'

'Exactly!' said Aunty Pussy.

'And what about your son, *ji*?'

'My son doesn't have streaks.'

'Your son doesn't have any hair to put streaks in.'

'Are you saying Jonkers is losing his hair?'

'*Losing? Losing?* Has lost. Is bald. Is loser. Has a failed marriage behind him and a belly in front of him. How do you expect my daughter to find him decent girls?'

'Your daughter couldn't find a decent girl even if the girl slapped her in the face.'

'Then why are you asking her? Calling her thousand-thousand times a day and eating her head and drinking her blood.'

'Because I want to give her empty, boring life some meaning.'

'Empty? Boring? She has house, social life, money,

servants, status, cars, jewellery. What more can anyone want? And she also has husband and child. You are just jealous. You've always been jealous. Even in school you were jealous. I remember how you took out the eyes of my dolly that Daddy got from Bombay. Because I had a dolly and you didn't. You've always been like that – jealous, sour, mean and nasty.'

'Jealous of *you*? That's a joke. Married to a nobody, a servant in someone else's business. Didn't even have his own factory,' sniffed Aunty Pussy.

'It wasn't an ordinary factory,' shrieked Mummy. 'It was a multinationalist with busy-busy factories in Jakarta and Africa and big-big offices in America and London. And he was an officer, not a servant, an officer with a tie and briefcase. Which your thief-tax-collector-embezzler husband couldn't become even if he tried for a thousand years. And by the way, the tax collector's proposal came first for me and only when I turned it down, because he was too poor and bore and ugly, did his mother come for you. Second-hand.'

'Don't make me open my mouth,' screamed Aunty Pussy. 'As if your upright husband with his briefcase and his tie hadn't been caught with the till in his paws, I mean, paws in the till. You've forgotten how he was almost thrown out by the big multinationalist company? And how his membership of Sindh Club was almost cancelled had it not been for my husband pleading with the governor then? Forgotten all that? Lost your memory now, have you?'

'You know, you've always been petty and mean and I don't want to talk to you. Ever!' shouted Mummy.

'Same here!' shouted Aunty Pussy.

And they both slammed phones, and now I'm not looking for girl for Jonkers and Mummy's told me to turn my back on him if I see him at any dinner-shinner (not that he's ever invited to any), and to forget I ever had an aunt called Pussy.

So I'm not looking for girl for Jonkers. Till at least tomorrow, when Mummy and Aunty Pussy will make out and then both of them will be on my case to find Jonkers a girl again. But at least I have one day off.

April 2006

So much of fun these weddings are. And thanks God
the heat is holding off a bit, which means that I don't
have to go dressed as a Hindu widow in white muslin.
In fact, one shouldn't blow too hard on one's own
drum, but I went as Ashwariya Rai in green contact
lenses and green satin sari with blue sequence.
Everyone said I looked splitting copy of her: Mummy,
Aunty Pussy and, er – Mummy and even Aunty Pussy,
who doesn't do anyone's praise for free. I had agreed
to take Jonkers along to spot nice-nice girls for
prospectus wives.

First I went to Humair's wedding, *na*. You know, to
Maha Rehman. Shaheema and Tariq Rehman's daughter,
only. There was a musical evening at Shaheema's. Very
tasteful, very nice.

Even Janoo didn't complain for once. In fact,
he's been singing Shaheema's praises. 'Instead of
feeding the fat cats of Lahore, she's given the money
she would have spent on the wedding to the

earthquake victims. She's put her money where her mouth is.'

I wanted to tell him if he'd put his money in my account I'd also put my mouth there, but then I thought maybe silent is golden. He's in a good mood so rarely these days that there's no need to take risks for nothing. So I put one rock on my heart and a bigger one around my neck (the emerald that The Old Bag gave me at our engagement – first and last nice thing she ever gave me) and went off to Meher Sethi's wedding.

What a spread! What organisation, what decoration (I think so professionals did it), what food, what drink! So big-hearted, so splashy. I have to admit, I was *tau* totally swept up.

'*Bus*,' I said to Janoo, 'I will do a same-to-same wedding for Kulchoo. No expense spared. You just wait and see, I will—'

'No. We'll do what Shaheema's done. We'll celebrate, of course, with a few close friends, but nothing lavish. We'll give the money away instead.'

Trust Janoo to pour water over all my plans. But I have also decided with myself that I'm not going to get into a you-you-me-me kind of argument with him. Instead I will try to be all sweet and understanding on top but inside I will do exactly what I want. Which is to have a HUUUUUGE wedding.

'Absolutely, darling. So clever you are, so sober, so bo— I mean, committed,' I cooed. 'We'll have a quiet little wedding and we'll send money for hundreds of poors to be fed at Data Sahib's shrine, but for the party before we'll get J&S to do a Mittal-type function with Indian stars and elephants at a French chatto like Where Sigh, except that I'll request the event managers to make one right here in Gulberg only, in the empty plot by Mummy's house, and invite about 1,000 of my closest friends. That way we'll give to charity also and get into *Good Times* also with Wedding of the Year and all your sober, sedate, bore friends will also say that just look at them, so much of responsibility they've shown by giving so much away. And who knows, maybe we can even get into the *Friday Times* with an article about our philan-trophy and perhaps even a profile of you. How about that, hmm?'

May 2006

I've just come, *na*, from Billoo's graduation in Boston.
He went to some place called U-Mess. He did law-
shaw or something like that. Who is Billoo? You may
well ask. He's Janoo's nephew. Son of Janoo's older
sister, Cobra, whom I hate less than only one other
person in the world – her sister, Psycho. So why did
I go? To keep an eye on Janoo, in case he looses his
mind and gives thousands of dollars as graduation
present. You never know with him, *na*.

And just as well I went because when Janoo gave
me the envelope to keep in my handbag that he was
going to present to Billoo after his ceremony, I saw
that it was bulging alarmingly. So I said excuse me
and pretended I needed to go and do small bathroom.
I nipped around the corner and carefully opened the
envelope to find ten 100-dollar notes lying all crisp-
crisp inside. I immediately took out five notes and
shoved them into my bra. Then I thought, Janoo
shouldn't get suspicious that envelope has become too

thin. So I counted out five one-dollar notes and I slid them inside instead.

Janoo may have forgotten, but I remember that we have a son called Kulchoo: and soon we'll have to pay his college fees, and get him married, and build him an annexe to our house, and buy him his first car, and then his first house, and also pay for his servants, and his children's school fees, and groceries and petrol and all. And God knows how expensive petrol will be then. And anyways, if you ask me 500 is also too much for Billoo. But if I took out more than that Cobra might report. This way she will think maybe Janoo gave only 505 dollars and stay quiet.

The risk was worth taking because as soon as bore graduation ceremony was over, I rushed to Macy in Boston and bought three pairs of shoes – one silver, one gold and one silver-and-gold. Then I also got some MAC lipsticks and D&G sent and La Prarry face cream and Landcombe mascara, and it all came to so little that I felt sorry for myself and so shopped some more from Billoo's graduation money. I told Janoo that honestly, shopping is best in America, and they so want you to have a nice day that you can't possibly disappoint them, no? Thanks God we didn't have to stay with Cobra in Boston for more than three days.

From there we came straight to London, and *uff*, it

was so hot, so hot that I thought I was going to pass out. Neither was there any air-con, no cooler, nor anything. Honestly, London is so backwards. Saw *Da Vinci's Coat*. Such a bore film. It's about some train or rail or something that's holy and everyone wants it. Stuppid . . .

June 2006

Got back to Lahore from London last week. *Uff*, it's hot, so hot that don't even ask. Too hot to think, to talk, to write. And this despite of air-conning night and day.

July 2006

Janoo is such an embarrassment also. He's so out of it. So untrendy, so uncaring, so behind when it comes to knowing what's hot and what's not. Take Mulloo's party yesterday.

Talking of Mulloo, I'm sooooo jay of her and Tony's new car. It's a bright red Porch. Mulloo looks a bit – shouldn't say, what with her being my best friend and all – but she looks so strange, so bazaar sitting in such a hot car with her *hijab* flapping in the wind. She tells me she's put a little book of holy prayers in the car, and she also does special prayers and blows on the car every morning because people look with so much of envy at them when they come roaring out of their house – which is just beside that huge open sewer with its rotten eggs and big-bathroom smells.

She tells me also that although she's constantly shooing them away when they have to stop at traffic lights, beggar children keep putting their dirty hands on the windows and Tony's had to send for a special non-bleach glass-cleaning spray just for cars only all the way from London. They've also had a porch built for the Porch right in front of their sitting room where the old lawn used to be, so when they are entertaining, all the guests can see the car – all gleaming and spot-lit and everything out of the big-big glass windows – with the big, gleaming swimming pool behind. I think so it's a bit show-offy and vulgar of them but then you know, *na*, that unlike me Mulloo didn't go to Kinnaird College. She is a Home Econmics girl. So what can you expect?

So I was telling you about the dinner party. Janoo was banging on and on about mangoes and how much he loves old varieties like Dussehris and Langras and another one called Summer Bewitched or something. People there were looking so bored and I *tau* was just dying with embarrassment, *na*. So I said, with a light, tinkly little laugh, 'Mangoes are so over, Janoo.'

'What do you mean?' he asked. 'The season's very much on.'

'She doesn't mean over,' added Mulloo, laughing in a not-so-tinkly-way, 'she means OVER! As in unfash-ionable. As in past-it. We *tau* just eat rambutan from Al-Fatah only, flown in fresh from Bangcock. Not so expensive. Just 800 rupees a kilo. So much nicer than mangoes, which I find so smelly, if I'm to be honest.

And talking of smells, you know that jasmine that grows in your garden, darling,' she said, turning to me. 'I thought it was so cute. So quaint!'

'What's quaint about jasmine?' asked Janoo, looking puzzled. 'For me it signifies summer.'

'How sweet,' Mulloo murmured. 'Depends where you spend your summers. For us summers are just orchids.'

'Tell me, Mulloo,' I said finally, 'when are you going to learn to swim? After all, you've had your pool for what, five years now?'

August 2006

Uff, it's so hot, so hot, I *tau* swear Janoo's brain has melted. A total crack *tau* he always was but now he's gone and got start staring mad. Such strange-strange things he's started doing. First he went and sold the Suzuki in which I sent the cook to buy groceries in the bazaar, saying we didn't need four-four cars and that it was polluting the air needlessly. Then he started switching off lights in empty rooms. And now he refuses to let me have my bedroom air-con on when I'm not there. Imagine! In this heat! Can you think of a bigger injustice? First I thought it must be tripping. The air-con, not Janoo.

I'd just come back from lunch at Mummy's and when I entered my room, I got such a blast of Saharan heat that I nearly got knocked up. So first I called the servants and screamed at them, but they said they didn't know anything, and then I called Shareef the electrician, who is crook number one it turns out. He hummed and hawed over it and said maybe it's the coolant, maybe the heatant, maybe the oppressor (or was it compressor?) or maybe just the dictator. Anyways, he charged me a thou but he got it going.

When Janoo came home I told him what had happened and first his face turned purple, then maroon, then red. Then he said, 'Did you not bother to have a look at that infernal machine yourself?'

'In case you haven't noticed, I'm not an electrician or a mechanic or something, okay?'

'Had you bothered to look you'd have realised that it was merely switched off.'

'*Switched off?*' I shrieked. 'You know I only switch it off in October.'

'Well, I did it today,' said Janoo. And then he started saying such weird-weird things that I nearly passed away. Apparently, at least according to Janoo, there is someone called Paula who has an ice-cap which has melted. Now if you will wear ice-caps in summers what do you expect? And then they say we Asians have silly fashions! Then he started ranting about some Global Warning that I think so someone has given. Must be Americans only. One day they are giving warning to Saddam, next day to Osama, then to Iran and now to that His Mullah or someone. And then on top he said there was climate change and that my little Suzuki and my air-con-until-October-habit were to blame. Listen to him! As if I'm, God forbid, God, or someone who can change climates.

But Mummy always told me that when men go mad, always look as if you agree with them and then go and do just the opposite. So I said yes, I know it's all my fault, but if you don't mind I'd like to change the climate in my room to winters, and so saying I turned my air-con on to terminal cool.

September 2006

Thanks God summers are over, well almost, and season has started, well almost. First there was that nice Munir and Bilal wedding in Lahore. I went on all seven days. So much of fun. And bride's outfit was totally gorge. Then there was Ali and Gillo Afridi's son's wedding in Isloo. Too, too fantastic with all that colour being flung all over the place and all the planes-loads of Karachiites all black and blue. Just like they celebrate Holi in Bollywood films. I think so they got the idea from there only.

Gillo and Ali have been living in Dubai forever. Actually even before forever – from olden days when Dubai-*wallahs* used to come for shopping to Karachi. Imagine!

Janoo of course didn't go to a single day of a single wedding. He is still in morning for Akbar Bugti, that political leader who was the head of the Bugti tribe in Balochistan, whom the army killed, *na*, and then pretended he'd died himself only. He wouldn't listen to the generals, and had taken refuse in a cave in the dessert. So they came after him with helicopters and bombs and things, and then they said his cave had fallen down on him in Balochistan and he'd died of natural becauses. Apparently not just the Bugtis but all of Balochistan is up in arms against Musharraf now.

But what's to Janoo? He's not even Baloch, let alone a Bugti. But when I said so to him that day he said, 'It's not just Bugti I'm morning, it's my country. You can go and dance your feet off if you want, but with Balochistan in flames I can't find all that much to celebrate.'

'*Haw*, *tau* what's happened to the fire engines?' I asked. 'Why can't they put out the flames in your precious Balochistan?'

He gave me a look and sank down into deep silence. I've *tau* been saying for the longest time that he is depress. All he talks of is Afghanistan and His Mullah and Gaza and someone else called Helmand, and how the Bugtis – man, woman, child – are on the Exist Control List, and Global Warning and God knows what else.

I swear, I should get a medal the size of a frying pan for putting up with him without going start staring mad. Aunty Pussy says I should get Victoria Crossed.

But Mummy says no, I deserve the Noble Prize for Peace. Like Nelson Mandela and Mother Theresa.

Till that happens, I've decided I'm going to resolve a Prozac into Janoo's tea every morning. It's that or pop one myself.

October 2006

Thanks God, Ramzan will finish before proper party season starts. Otherwise all the weddings, all the parties, everything would have had water poured over them. *Haw*, maybe I shouldn't have said that. Everyone is saying the Muslim God is wrathful. What if I'm stuck down now? Please Allah, sorry, sorry, didn't mean that, *na*. Please don't it take personally, okay? I mean, if it wasn't for this nice month-long rest that you force on us every year when would I get the time to get my party wardrope sorted, hmm? And my manicure and pedicure done? And my highlights put? And just to show You how sorry I am, I'm going to have a nice big fast opening for the poors, in Your name only. I hope You are going to give me lots of credit points in the after-life for opening fast of so many people. And send me straight to heaven, hmm? But only when I die, and not before, okay?

But what to do? I don't know any poors. At least not since I discovered that Janoo's cousin Shameless (well, her real name's Shama), who I used to take pity on because her husband's hardwear shop had gone bust and who I used to think was hand-to-mouth and who I used to give all my worn shoes to, turned out to have won some huge lottery in Calgary, Canada and was the proud owner of not one, not two, but three flats there. Anyways, with that snake-in-the-grass Shameless a millionaire, I don't know any more poors. My servants, who are all fat as bufallows and have big-big TV sets in their quarters, don't count as poors obviously. But I suppose if all my guests bring their drivers then I could open their fasts and get all my bonus points, couldn't I? So now I must make sure no one drives their own car.

I'll have to tell Tony not to bring his Porch Roadstir in that case. He *tau* won't even let his driver put his little finger on it, except to clean of course. And also I'll have to persuade Janoo before I can do fast-opening parties. He hates them, you know, *iftaar* parties. He says it's just an orgy of eating and self-righteous opining and he's had it with self-righteous opining after reading Musharraf's new thriller, *In the Land of Fire*.

He thinks Mush has gone too far, revealing all the beggings and pleadings US did with him after 9/11 and it's only a matter of time now before the Americans organise a little plane crash for him too. *Hai*, please don't speak like that, I said to Janoo: at least let me have my *iftaar* party before we all go up in flames.

In any case, I really don't know why Janoo is after Mush the whole time. He's given us so many TV channels and pop groups and so many fashion shows and so many mobile phones, we should get down on our feet and thank him. Has any democratic leader ever given this much? And so what if he's a general who took us by force? And so what if he's not elected? Did I elect The Old Bag to be my mother-in-law? Sometimes you just have greatness thrust upon you, and then you just have to grin and bear it. So I'm grinning and Janoo's bearing.

November 2006

Mark Lyall-Grant is going, *na*. You know, the British High Commissioner. So lots of bye-bye parties are happening in Isloo, Karachi and here. I wanted to take my passport to the one here so that he could quickly give me five-year multiple-entry visa to London, so I don't have to gravel at the Brit High Commission in Isloo till at least 2010. But Janoo said I was crack. One, he doesn't give visas. Then who gives, I asked? The consular people, he said.

'*Haw*, the local council? Now *they* are giving? Must have given bribes left, right and centre to get the stamp from British High Commission.'

Janoo looked heavenward and shoved me into the car. So rude, he is. No manners, no curtsy, no good brought-up. But what can you expect with The Old Bag for a mother? Not like my Mummy, who always taught me to keep my little finger up in the air when holding a teacup and always flushing first before sitting on toilet in other people's homes so they can't hear you actually doing small bathroom.

'Do you know Lyall-Grant's father founded Lyallpur?' Janoo asked me on the way to the party.

'Really?' I said, twisting the rearview mirror to my side to check my new Landcombe Rogue Noir lipstick. 'When did it get lost?'

Janoo heaved another sigh and snatched the rearview mirror back to his side. As I said, no brought-up he has.

December 2006

Have ordered five new designer outfits in preparation
for the up-and-coming wedding season. Two from
Kami, two from Sonia Batla and one from Hasan
Sheheryar, and I'll kill you if you tell Janoo. Not that
it's any of his business because I've not touched a
penny of his. Kulchoo had them made for me. That's
right, Kulchoo! My own little shweetoo darling boy.
Why? Because he loves me and wants to see me
happy. At least that's what he wrote in his school
essay, 'I want my Mummy and Daddy to be happy.'
So I thought, then he won't mind if I sell that little
gold brick that The Old Bag gave him for his last
birthday. Anyways, what's he going to do with a gold
brick, hmm? Whereas I, I could get a Hasan Sheheryar,
a Kami, a Batla and live happily ever after – at least
till the end of the month. I think so I'll wear the
Kami to one day in Sanam Taseer's wedding. I hear
it's going to be a fab celebration over two weeks,
with party and disco and reception and *mehndi* and

dinner with a thousand guests at each event, and then all of it all over again in the pages of *Good Times* to gloat over. *Uff*, so much of fun!! Janoo says I've become a fixture in *Good Times*. Between you, me and the four walls, I've started recognising their photographer, *na*, and any time I spot him at a party or gallery opening or ball or whatever, I immediately pout and make sure I am standing inside his camera lens. After all, one has to paddle one's own canoe in life, otherwise who else is going to do it for you?

But I hope it won't go and rain and spoil everything. That will be so bore. It's good it's happened now only – rain, for heaven's sake, what else? I think so some bits of Karachi and Lahore even have become so flooded that people have been macarooned in their houses. But I think so only in poor-poor bits of the city. In posh areas like Defence, Gulberg and GOR, thanks Almighty Allah, everyone is warm and dry and partying away.

Talking of Karachi, I hear Shobha Day came there to launch a new novel by Nadia A. R. It's called *Kolachi Dreams* and if it's juicy and filled with all the things I love most – goss and clothes and parties, then tau I will gobble it up. Maybe I should write one myself. I'll call it *Lahori Nights* – or no, *Lahori Days*. One should be original, no? Otherwise all those jay types like Mulloo, Maha and all will say I've stolen the idea from someone else. As if I'm some copycat or cheater-cock or something.

January 2007

Janoo and Kulchoo have gone off without even breathing a word to me. They've gone of all places to bore Sharkpur. They've decided to bunk the wedding season and go off to – what does Janoo call it? – yes, 'presume with nature'. It's just a show-off way of saying that he's a loser who wanders through muddy fields and drinks enormous mugs full of smelly bufallow milk. (Thanks God for Nestlay milk, I say, which comes in nice clean cartons which smell only of cardboard. No more stinky cows for me.)

Anyways, going back to Janoo, I could have boasted about him a little, about how he's manly and blood-thirsty, if he'd had the grace to do at least some hunting-shunting. But no! He won't do that even. Wildlife, he says, is on the verge of distinction and the only shooting he'll do is with a camera. As if he's Mahesh Bhatt or Steven Spellburg or something! All Kulchoo could talk about was having seen a fallow deer in the wild. Honestly! Janoo can be what Janoo wants, but why did he have to go and make my poor old son into a bucket case also? And he's going to become so black also, from wandering outside all day.

'Well,' I responded, 'I may not be one of your precious fallow deers, but it may interest you to know that I was also on the verge of distinction from worrying about you. At least you could have told me.'

'But, Mama,' said Kulchoo, 'we made the plan on the spur of the moment when you were at the hair-dresser's. We called your mobile but you probably couldn't hear over the blow-dryer. I even left a message but you never called back so I thought you were okay with our trip.'

Hmm. I remember dimly seeing a missed call from Janoo but since I knew it was going to be some bore complaint or the other, I never checked. But of course I couldn't admit that, so I started screaming and shouting about how the message never came and then Janoo said he'd show me his mobile to show the exact time and date when Kulchoo had made the call. And so I shouted even louder about how no one trusts me and no one cares how I feel, and how embar-rassed I was having to lie to Naz and Mansha about how Janoo was ill in bed and so couldn't attend Hassan's fab wedding reception, and how I'd had to hitch a ride with Mulloo to Naila Haq's New Year party like some poor car-less person, and how I'm getting late for Bunny and Sarmad's wedding reception now and don't have the time to stand around arguing with two bucket-case losers anyways . . .

February 2007

God is on my side. I've always known, but now it's official. If He hadn't been, then He wouldn't have ended Muharram in time for Basant, now would He? So all the *mullahs* and other kill-joys can go fly a kite. Oh, sorry, forgot! They can't fly a kite because they belief it's anti-Islamic. Their Islamic marriages will break, or some such thing, if they do so much as look at a kite. Well, they can go and do whatever it is that they do, because I *tau* damn care, frankly speaking.

So in keeping with Basant theme and its yellow colour code, I'm all ready with my sunflower-gold outfit. Last year I had lemon-yellow one and the year before that butter-yellow and the year before that a sort of jaundice-yellow and the year before that mustard and the year before that – I've forgotten. Anyways, point is one should keep changing, *na*, otherwise people think you are struck in a grove and they start taking you for granted and once people start taking you for granted then you might as well give up.

278

So this time, knowing that surprise is best element of attack, I've also had my hair dyed a sort of sunflower-yellow to keep up the surprise elements.

Now I'm all set for Basant. Let the countdown begin . . .

March 2007

Two days. Just two measly days of fun and parties.
And then over! Everything finish, everything over.
Shutters down. Lights out. Gates locked. Everyone go
home. So unfair. So selfish. So spoil-spot. Who? The
fundos, who else?

They went and shortened Basant from one week to
two days. Can you imagine? It comes after a whole
year and then we can only celebrate for two days. And
why? Because it is un-Islamic. Kite-flying is un-Islamic,
they say. Well, what is Islamic then? Cricket? Hockey?
Did they used to play that back then? Bedminton?
Football? And what about riding in cars and planes?
The *mullahs* should ride on camels then. And what
about rocket launchers? And Cruise missiles? Did they
use that for doing *jihad* back then? No, they had arrows
and swords. So let them fight the Americans with
arrows and swords in Afghanistan. Why do they use
bombs then? Bloody hippo-crits, liars. I *tau* tell you,
am so fed up. So up to here with their constant lectures

and sermons. The minute they see someone having a bit of fun they come down on them like a Cruise missile. Reminds me of Kulchoo's Monopoly: 'Go to jail, go directly to jail. Do not pass Go. Do not collect £200. Kill-joys. Hippo-crits. Bores. Losers.

But one good thing the beardos have done. They've brought Janoo and me together. Yes, promise by God. They've done the impossible. This is what happened: I came back from the second day's parties – you know, Izzat Majeed's do at his farm and Asif Jah's *haveli* function and, of course, a quick hello-hi at Yusuf's and Bali's farm thing at Bedian, where incidentally Mush also came – and came home and wrenched my yellow stilettos off and hurled them across the room.

Janoo, who as usual was sitting reading some bore book, looked up and said mildly, 'Anything the matter?'

So I started abusing the fundos, of course. At this he put his book down, crossed his arms across his chest and said, 'Do I see the stirrings of a political consciousness here?'

'I don't know what you see but I can tell you how I feel. FED UP. So fed up, so fed up that don't even ask. I mean, why can't the beardos go off to some island like Green Land or Bermuda or something and make their own bore kingdom for themselves, where no one is allowed to laugh or fly a kite or sing a song or wear sleeveless?'

'Might be a bit nippy to go sleeveless in Green Land. Global warming notwithstanding,' Janoo murmured.

'What? Who's without standing? What are you talking about?'

'Nothing,' he said hurriedly. 'Go on.'

'Why can't they just go off and leave us alone to pay for our own sins and to answer Allah ourselves? It's not as if I'm asking anyone else to jump into the fires of hell for me, am I? So why can't they leave us alone?'

At this he looked at me in wonder and said, 'Madam, I salute you!' And then he took me out to dinner. At Cosa Nostra Restaurant. Candlelight. Roses. Bliss.

April 2007

So much of trouble poor Gen Mush is in. And why?
Because he threw out a judge. Big bloody deal. People
throw their husbands and wives out and nobody turns
a hare, so what's all this fuss for a judge, hmm? I think
so it's very unfair the way they are taking out rallies
every day and going on strikes at the drop of a bat
and generally being so mean to poor old General Mush.

Quite apart from the fact that I haven't been able
to go down the Mall for a little bit of Thai food at
Royal Elephant – that soup of theirs, I forget its name,
is sooo delish – because of the processions that these
spoil-spot lawyers are taking out every other day, I
really think that they should show a little bit of curtsy
to a man who's allowed us fashion shows and satter-
light TV and New Year's Eve parties. I mean, it's not
like General Mush was like General Zia or something,
who wouldn't let us wear sleeveless and dance at New
Year's, you know? Honestly, Mush is my favourite
general. So nice he is. You should ask the Indians,

they're so jay of us for having him. And that nice Shock Aziz with his nice, silken voice and his nice, silken manners and his nice, silken suits. Honestly, that's our problem, never give enough thanks to Allah.

As usual, I had a big fight with Janoo about it. Yes, I can hear you say, what's new? What's new is that we hadn't fought for a while. Part of the reason is that he was in Sharkpur for ten days – so he wasn't there to fight with – but part of the reason was also that we were not talking since our last fight. But anyways, we had a big fight over Mush and cricket.

Janoo, of course, is behaving as if the sacked judge was his own father and is taking it all very personally, and when I said, 'So what's the big deal?' I thought he was going to have a heart attack like poor old Bob Woolmer. And he said if our team played with even half the commitment with which they pray, then maybe we could win ten World Cups. And I said that he was just sour because he'd bought a new wall-mounted TV for the World Cup and after our undignified exit and our dead coach now he has to watch Australia win in double size.

Actually, poor old Mulloo and Tony had booked tickets and made hotel reservations and everything for the World Cup, and had been show-offing for the last three months about how they were off in the first week of April to watch Pakistan win the cricket World Cup in Caribian. And now they have gone all quiet and the goss is that they are trying to get their money back and can't. Serves them right for being so cheap!

Anyways, I said to Kulchoo, why didn't he buy a book or something for his father that he could read to forget his sorrows about cricket and Bob Woolmer. And he said when had I started subscribing books as remedies to people given that I never read myself? So I said what nonsense he was talking.

And he said, 'Go on, then, name one book you know well.'

And cool as a cucumber, I said, 'Cheque book!'

May 2007

I went. Janoo went. Kulchoo went. So did Mummy, Daddy, Aunty Pussy, Maha, Sunny, Baby and Mulloo-and-Tony. Even Jonkers went. Where? Oh for heaven's sake! Where are you? To the anti-fundo rally of course. On April 14th in Lahore. Everyone I know went. Yes, yes, I know, I'm not the rallying type and yes, I know you think I did it only for getting my pictures in papers, but you can think whatever you want, because I damn care. I know why I went, and that's all that matters. So why I went?

I went because enough is enough, okay? For the last twenty years, ever since bloody Zia, I've been turning a blind cheek and the other eye. At first I thought if the fundos want to grow beards and carry Kalashnikovs and wear their *shalwars* short to show off their hairy ankles, and put their women in *burqas* and their sons in *madrassahs*, so let them. What goes of mine? They want to go and fight in Kashmir, let them. They want to die in Afghanistan,

let them. Live and let live – or in this case, die –
I thought.

But it's not like that. Because the fundos are not
prepared to live and let us live. They are control freaks.
Like class monitors, they want to tell us when we can
talk and when we can't. When we can go to toilet and
when we can't. When we can sit down and when we
can't. Today they are saying that I can't wear sleeveless
and must cover my head. Tomorrow they will say I
must cover my face. Then they will say that even
behind my *niqab* I can't wear make-up. Then they will
say I can't even wear lipstick at home, or cut my hair,
or wear sent, or paint my nails. Then they will say I
can't drive. And nor can I sit in a car alone with a
driver to whom I am not related by blood. Then they
will say I can't go in mixed company. So I can't go to
Al-Fatah to do my shopping, or go to Dynasty Chinese,
or even to Tariq Amin's for my highlights and facial.

Parties will be completely out. Not even GTs will
be allowed, so you can forget balls. Also going to
London, Dubai, Singapore, New York it will all be
band. Then they will say I can't read English books
or watch movies or listen to songs. Not even family-
type soaps like *Kyonke Saas Bhi Kabhi Bahu Thi*.
Then they will say I can't inherit property. So Daddy's
house and all his shares and all will go to his brother's

sons and all I'll inherit from him will be his blood pressure and diebeetes. Then they will say Janoo can marry however many times he wants, and I can't say no to him. Then they will say I can't die-vorce him. And if I don't do as they say, then they will say that I am asking for it, and they will march me to a stadium and, in front of thousands of other beardo control freaks who will all be cheering like mad, they will behead me. So you see, I can't stay unbothered. THAT'S why I went to the march. Because I've realised there's no turning a blind eye with fundos. Because they won't let you.

June 2007

Mulloo came to my house on the day before I was leaving for London – packing-shacking, everything was done – and said, '*Haw*, are you crack or something, going to London?'

'Why?' I asked. 'Why am I crack?'

'Everyone who's come from there says it's hotter than Africa there and no air-cons and no ceiling fans even. So behind they are, *na*. We went last year in the summers and swore we'd never go in the summers again. This year we're going to Thailand, where everything, even the swimming pool, is air-conned. My *tau* shoe even wouldn't go to London in summers. Not even if you paid it, *baba*.'

But thanks God, I didn't listen to Mulloo. She is just jay. Tony is in trouble with the banks, *na*. They are calling in their loans and Tony is playing hide and seek all over the place with them. The Porch is gone and so is the second Prado. And last week I saw Mulloo's diamond earrings – the three-carrot drop – at

Goldsmith's. She pretended they'd come to be fixed but Iqbal Sahib told me himself only that she's asking sixty *lakhs* for them and 'not a *paisa* less'. So I think so they can't afford London and that's why the poor things, they are having to make do with Phookit. Maybe they can't even cuff up the twenty-five thou fee for the British visa.

But we can, and it's so nice here in London. So cool-cool, so breezy-breezy. A bit of rain and Janoo keeps complaining and grumbling that he can't see Wimbledong but I *tau* damn care. But if you ask me, I think so the monsoon has come here also. Apparently in their Northern Areas there's been proper flooding-shlooding. Places like Badford and Leads and God knows where else. Where their Talibans types live. You know, the *ninjas* in their *burqas* and trainers and the *mullahs* with their beards down to their knees, who say, '*Salaam aleikum, innit?*' Them only.

But why spoil my holidays by thinking about all of that bore stuff? Particularly when so many nice types from decent baggrounds are here these days. At Deutsche Bank's annual Subcontinentals' party last week there were Naseem and Sehyr Saigol from Lahore, Saira Lakhani from Karachi, Qadir Jaffer, Gillo Afridi, and also I hear Habib Fida Ali is here and Mian Sheheryar also, and Meliha and Sikander are coming and Monty and Amina have just gone and Popity is coming and so are Irfan and Gullie. *Hai*, so much fun, just like a huge Lahori GT in London. And poor Mulloo is sitting all by herself in boring old Phookit . . .

July 2007

Look at MQM! Look at Musharraf! Look at the army! Look at all these stuppid district councillors who pushed all their hungry-naked types into buses and dragged them all the way to Isloo for Musharraf's tit-for-tit rally with the lawyers and judges. Shame on them! Stuppids! Not the poors, the councillors. Honestly, there must be some limit to shamelessness, no? It's like Mulloo inviting me to tea and then expecting me to bring my servants to serve. And bringing all the eats as well. And me going along doing 'Yes, Mulloo, of course, Mulloo, whatever you say Mulloo' like a total shameless and taking all my servants along in a trailer holding samosas and cakes.

Talking of Islamabad, I heard on Al Jazeera last night that guvment has finally blitzed the Lal Masjid crazies. But why be all lovey-dovey and allowing them to burn as many video shops as they like and

terrorise as many citizens as they like for not wearing
beards or covering themselves in the first place
then? Why promise to rebuild their mosques and
let them have run of Islamabad as if it were their
father's own private estate, hmm? Janoo says Mush
has lost the plot. Which one, I said? A four-star
general like Mush be receiving so many. And not
just residential plots but agricultural lands also. In
Sharkpur all of the biggest landowners are now
retired generals if you please, all of whom received
acres and acres of the best agricultural lands as a
goodbye present.

I tell you, the Chief Justice of the Supreme
Court is my new hero. Shame he doesn't look more
like Brad Pitts, but he's still my hero. Janoo is one
minute up, one minute down, just like the mouse
in the clock. At first he was so excited, so excited
that don't even ask. He kept banging on about the
reassertion of civil society. He took part in every
single demonstration, in every single protest in
Lahore, and wrote hundred-hundred letters to the
newspapers also, asking for Chief Justice to be
reinstalled. But now he says lawyers are beginning
to act like a political party. They are electioneering
instead of lawyering.

'Just make up your mind,' I said, 'instead of running up and down the clock.'

He looked at me puzzled. I think so he didn't understand my illusion to the mouse in the clock. Poor thing, he is not poetry-minded like me.

But it was poor Jonkers, really, who got it in the neck. He was in Karachi that day, *na*, when CJ was expected to give speech there in a big rally but wasn't allowed to step into the city by MQM, which has always been in the back pocket of the army *na*. That's when MQM decided to silence all the protestors and cow all their critics in Karachi by unleashing terrible violence. So what was I saying? Yes, Jonkers in Karachi: Aunty Pussy has a plot just on the backside of Drigh Road which she's been wanting to sell for ages and she'd sent him to find buyers for it. So anyways, you know that Jonkers never reads the papers and on TV also he only watches the film channel, so he didn't know CJ was expected in Karachi. So he arrived at the plot where he had appointment with a state agent and he waited and waited but no one came. He said the streets were a bit quietish and a bit emptyish and also a bit spookyish and he started feeling a bit worried.

For a moment or two he even considered

going home but then the thought of Aunty Pussy's rage was even more scary, so he stood and stood but still the state agent wouldn't come, wouldn't come. Finally he saw a motorbike coming slowly towards him, and he was so reliefed to see someone at last that he was about to run and throw his arms around them, but as the motorbike got closer he saw there were two men and one had the lower half of his face covered by a handkerchief, like, you know, thiefs and murderers in cowboy films, and the other was carrying a Kalashnikov and looking as bloodthirsty as Dracula, honest by God.

Jonkers *tau* poor thing was so terrified that he dived into the bushes of his old house and sat there hunched up, shivering and shaking like Aunty Pussy's upper arms. Luckily the motorcycle-*wallahs* didn't see him. But he saw everything. All the shootings and the murders and the firing and the killing that took place on that street that day. And the police standing to one side, picking their noses. He was there in the bush for nine hours, poor Jonkers. He's still suffering from trauma even though he's been safe at home now for three days. So shame on Musharraf, shame on MQM, shame on all the stuppids who did this to poor, decent Jonkers. And, oh yes, I must remember the poors who died also. Poor them.

August 2007

So sad. So, so, so sad. Such high hopes I had of Mush.
In fact, everyone had. Mulloo, Tony, Aunty Pussy,
Mummy, Sunny, Baby, even Jonkers, who, poor thing,
after his broken marriage had stopped being hopeful
altogether. And now Mush has gone and bashed all
our hopes. We never thought he'd go bonkers like this.

Only Janoo, kill-joy, in his usual doom and bloom
way, always said, 'Mark my words, however much he
might bang on about enlightened moderation and
however liberal and open he might seem, a general
is in the end a general. He doesn't know how to
share power.'

Between you, me and the four walls, I damn care
about power sharing, as long as he kept us happy
and rich. House prices were rising (ours is for ten
crores now, *mashallah*), international supermarkets
like Carry Four and Metro and all were coming to
Pakistan, Americans were happy with us, olive oil
was flowing in Al-Fatah, and after all these years of

visa constrictions and police reporting, hopping across to India to shop in Delhi's Khan Market had become so easy. What more does anyone want, hmm? Okay, I admit, there were a couple of little things, like that Red Mosque fiasco where he let the chicks with sticks hold all of Isloo to handsome for weeks and weeks before blasting them off the face of the earth, and then there was the stuppid move he made on the Chief Justice, sacking him as if he was Mush's own personal servant, but really, these are such small-small things when you compare them to the big-big things like house prices and all, that I feel that we should forgive and forget.

I said to Janoo when he was going on and on about Mush, 'Just look how much of freedom Mush gave to the press! Society mags like *Good Times*, chat shows like *Begum Nawazish Ali* and *Zainab Can't Cook*, *Sunday* . . .'

'The army must learn to let go,' he said. 'Musharraf is stifling civil society. And it won't work. It just won't work.'

'Maybe it's the heat,' I said. 'If air-cons are melting, maybe his brain is also melting.'

'His political system is certainly in meltdown,' said Janoo.

God knows who will come now. Benazir or Nawaz?

I am so sick of that silly ping-pong. They come, they loot, they go. One is sitting in big, fat flat in London and the other is sitting in big, fat flat in Dubai and talking from there only about what-what they will do, and how horrid Mush is and how lovely they are! And here we are all boiling in the heat with no electricity on top.

But one piece of good news. Now all the white cricket teams are saying Bob Woolmer died himself only and that nobody killed him. Look at them! After all those suspicious looks at our poor, pious, God-fearing players, and all that talk of match-fixing and poisoning and doing DMA testing of them and muttering-shuttering about bribery and corruption. Just because they have big beards and can't speak too much of English and throw the occasional match doesn't mean our boys are murderers. I tell you, it's just racism. If New Zealand's or Australia's coach had died, no one would have said a thing. Just because it's big, bearded, brown us . . . Honestly!

September 2007

Goss is – and not just flying-around, everyday goss, but real, reliable goss – that Mush was about to declare emergency but Condi Rice called in the middle of night and told him, 'Don't you dare!'

Apparently his finger was two inches away from emergency button when phone rang. 'Hello? Who's that?' he said.

'It's me only. Miss Condiment Rice. Listen, I'm telling to you that don't even think about it. Otherwise no one will be worst to you than us. And then don't say we didn't say. Okay? Now take your finger out and go to sleep. And when you wake up in the morning go and hunt Talibans.'

And phone went 'brrrmmm' after that.

But problem is, what is Mush to do? Janoo says Americans are saying, 'Go fetch Benazir Bhutto', but BB is also not agreeing. As Janoo says, she's no Sonia Gandhi willing to stay in the bagground and let someone from her party become PM. Not in a thousand million years. She'd rather put her dog on the PM's chair than any of her party members. Did you see the way she became so jay of her own party man, Aitzaz Ahsan, when he was all over the papers for fighting with Mush over the ouster of the Chief Justice? Janoo thought she was going to throw him out on his year then and there only. Also, if she doesn't become PM then how is she going to make more money? Between you, me and the four walls, it's a bit of a dialemma. So God alone knows who's going to come as PM next.

I'm ready to have anyone but the *mullahs*. Even Imran or Nawaz are better, but Janoo suspects they might be hand in gloves with the *mullahs*. What a cynic! So who to choose? Honestly!

Matric results have come. Our driver's son got second division pass. He was eating Janoo's head to get him a guvmunt job. Janoo did some sting-pulling and got him into Forests, but he says he wants Customs or Police and not a loser job with no money-making prospectus like Forests. Janoo's told him to go to hell.

Mulloo's back from Singapore with a suitcase full of shoes and bags. Maha's come back from New York with a new nose. She swears she's had nothing done, but in June her nose was a jacket potato and now it's a french fry. Honestly, so full of liars and cheaters this country is. No wonder we are an emergency . . .

October 2007

Look at them! Bursting bombs on Benazir's home-coming procession and killing so many peoples. You know yesterday I was watching TV late into the night because Janoo as you know, he is a news junky, *na*, and he wouldn't switch off the wall-mounted 48-inch screen in our bedroom which he got for World Cup, even though it was so late at night. And so I was also forced to watch, and one minute it was claps and cheers and drums and dance and the next, a loud bang and smoke and screams and bodies. Next day, as soon as we found out that it was a suicide bomb Janoo immediately announced that it was Al Qaeda.

'How you can be sure?' I asked.

'Because only ideological zealots blow themselves up,' he replied.

I wanted to ask him who is zealots, but you know he makes such tired faces when you ask him any questions that I thought, why to subject myself to his scorns? And anyways silent is golden.

Next day we went to Mulloo's for dinner and Janoo was saying what a relief it was that Benazir didn't get harmed, when Tony said, 'Typical! She herself survived and got so many innocent people killed. If you ask me, she has blood on her hands.'

'What?' Janoo asked, open-mouthed.

Oh God, I thought, now there is going to be a big, ugly argument. So quickly I said to Mulloo, 'Hai, Mulloo, your hair is looking so nice. You've had it dyed again?'

'What do you mean, "blood on her hands"?' asked Janoo in that soft-type voice he puts on just before he explodes.

'What are you talking about?' snapped Mulloo. 'My hair is naturally auburn.'

'So many times Musharraf had said, "Don't take out processions, don't take out processions because we can't guarantee your safety",' said Tony. '"Instead, go in helicopter." We know the risks because we know everything. But would she listen? Never! Stubborn to the last, just like her father.'

'If they knew the risks, why didn't they give her better security?' asked Janoo.

'It must be the light, then, Mulloo,' I continued desperately, 'because honestly your hair is looking almost carrot-coloured.'

'Problem is,' said Tony, leaning back in his leather

armchair and resting his huge glass of whisky on his paunch, 'these rich, corrupt politicians, what do they care about the poor man on the street? All they care about is votes. What does it matter to Benazir if 300, even 3,000 die? Unlike us ordinary folk, politicians don't care about the man on the street.'

'My hair is natural,' hissed Mulloo. 'I've told you a thousand-thousand times.'

'I don't believe it. I just don't believe it,' said Janoo. 'Instead of asking who has killed all these people and why, you are blaming the victim, or at least the intended victim. Have you gone mad?'

'If you are about to blame our God-fearing religious brothers then you can stop right now,' said Tony, slamming his glass down on the table.

'Who but a religious fanatic blows himself up? For what?'

'How should I know?' shrugged Tony. 'Maybe it was someone from within her own party.'

'How can that be?' I reasoned calmly with Mulloo. 'Your mother had black hair, your father black. How come you are red?'

'I am a redhead,' repeated Mulloo. 'Natural redhead, okay?'

'What nonsense, Tony!' scoffed Janoo. 'I never heard such bullshit in my life.'

'If we are so full of bullshit and also if you are going to make mean-mean jealous comments about our hair, then I think so we'd better part companies, no?' said Mulloo, with a tight smile.

'My thoughts exactly,' said Janoo, rising to his feet. 'Come!' he barked at me, as if I was a faithful labradog sitting at his feet.

But I couldn't even argue with him in front of Mulloo, *na*, because she'd be so happy to see us fight. So I followed him out with my nose in the hair. Tomorrow I'll send some flowers to her because she's having big New Year's party and my nose will be cut if I'm dropped from the invitation list. But I swear to God, she's had her hair dyed carrot. It's about as natural as Aunty Pussy's teeth.

November 2007

Yesterday I said to Janoo, 'Thanks be to Almighty Allah, holy month of Ramzan is almost finished, *mashallah*. Just one more week to go and then *bus*, by the grace of Almighty Allah, Eid *inshallah*.'

Janoo raised an eyebrow and said, 'Are you also growing a beard?'

I clapped my hand to my chin where only yesterday I'd had my sixth laser dose done. Turning my back on Janoo I quickly felt with my fingers, but no stubble. Not even one or two thorn-like things poking out. And just as well because I've already spent eighteen thou rupees on it, and I've still got two sessions to go. My chin was a bit sore, but definitely no stubble. So I swung back and glared at him.

'What do you mean, beard? I'll tell you who the bearded ladies are in your family . . .'

'Metaphorically,' Janoo said hurriedly. 'I was speaking metaphorically.'

'Stratospherically,' I replied at once. 'And I was speaking stratospherically.'

Yesterday only, Kulchoo was telling me that after earth there is stratosphere and it's very, very high, higher than Everest even. So I thought: time to show Janoo that I can also do high-high talk. Just because he's been to Oxford and is an Oxen, doesn't mean only he can use big-big words.

'Sorry?' he said.

'It's too late to be sorry,' I said, lifting my chin proudly. 'What's been said has been said.'

'Look, I don't know what you're going on about,' he said. 'I was just making a comment, albeit a facetious one, about your new-found piety, and wondering whether you too had become a fully paid-up member of the God squad. That's all!'

I think so Janoo's frightened of going to hell. He's seen me keeping all the fasts this year and saying all my prayers, even the middle-of-the-night ones. Actually he hasn't seen me too much lately, because he's been in Sharkpur where he's been interviewing teachers for his bore school, and I've been asleep in Lahore. (I go to bed after dawn, *na*, and don't wake till sunset, when it's time to open the fast. Then I do my four remaining prayers all in one lump sum, you know, because the Almighty is very understanding and forgiving *na* and then I go to Mulloo and Tony's for a GT or something, then I come home and watch DVDs till it's time for fast-keeping again.)

Janoo, of course, hasn't done a thing for the holy month of Ramzan. Not for a minute he's thought of praying or remembering God or anything. All month he's been sitting in his bore village in Sharkpur, where he's built a free school for children, and now he went to set up a library and fit in a computer and hire teachers and things. Imagine! And he doesn't even fight an election from there. Crack!

'It's not too late, you know,' I said. 'There's still a week to go. You can keep your fasts and Allah Almighty, the Merciful, the Beneficient, will forgive you.'

'You know something?' said Janoo, peering closely at my face. 'As you speak, I can actually see hairs sprouting from your chin . . .'

December 2007

So what's new? Hmm. Nawazu is back of course from his long exile in Saudi Arabia, and not in some broken-down PIA plane, which all smell of socks and lamb curry, but in King Abdullah's own gleaming golden plane, which probably reeks of attar of roses and serves Houbara bustard soup and ibex biryani. And then he rode home also in King Abdullah's own bulletproof Merc and he probably also called and thanked him from the bottoms of his heart the minute he got home for arranging everything so nicely. Not at all like last time he tried to come back to Lahore when Musharraf didn't even allow him to get off his plane! I tell you, it's always good to have friends in high places.

And Imran Khan's started eating again. He's no longer on hunger strike. And Mush has stopped being a general but I don't know how I'm going to recognise him now without his uniform and medals and stick. He's handed his army stick to General Kayani also so that *he* can beat us up now instead of Mush. And

Jemima has become expert on Pakistan. She's started making so many demonstrations in London and writing articles. The old PM, Shock Aziz, is on his way out – no Saudi plane for him, but. And Benazir? Who knows what BB's up to? At first I thought the Americans had forced Mush to join hands with her and bring democracy back to Pakistan, as if she was an estranged wife, but I think so now Mush and BB have had a separation. God knows who she will join hands with now. Nawaz? The Chaudhrys? Imran? The mullahs? MQM? The republicans? Maybe she's like those Indian goddesses with hundreds of hands that she can join with everyone at once without anyone knowing.

Janoo of course is shouting himself horse. 'We are not a sovereign nation!' he says. 'We're a joke! Americans are fielding their candidate, the Saudis theirs, the army is sitting on top of us, and we are getting crushed underneath.'

What else is happening? Elections are coming. Or so Mush says. We'll belief it when we see it. Meantime, inflation has become so much, so much that don't even ask. Servants are demanding pay rise. Look at them! They say they can't afford bread. So don't eat bread, I want to tell them. Eat rice. Or still better, cut out carbs altogether. Do Atkins, like me.

It was so nice and quiet when Janoo was gone. Gone where? *Haw*, don't you know? Janoo went to jail, *na*. High point of his life and you're asking where he went? He's sooo proud of himself for being arrested with 'like-minded, responsible citizens'. Oho, he got bundled into the same van as all those Human Rights Commission Pakistani-*wallahs na* – the Ali Cheemas, the Meena Rehmans, the Ahmed Hossains and the Bilal Mintos of Lahore. The litred, bore brigade. So proud he was of 'standing shoulder-to-shoulder with them'.

At first I got a bit worried when I heard he'd been locked up. I thought maybe he's been thrown into Attock or Mianwali jail or somewhere scary like that but when I heard he was sitting in Model Town only, with all those bore responsibles who are sure to make big fuss and get themselves out in the winking of an eye, then *tau* I relaxed and thought, I bet he's having nice time, and so should I. So *bus*, for next two days I had so much of massages and watched so many of DVDs – *Om Shanti Om*, *Desperate Housewives*, *Parineeta* again (*uff*, that one *tau* I just adore).

But then Janoo came back covered all over with mosquito bites and announced he was going to throw up Mush now. Just listen to him!

'Yes, Janoo,' I said. 'Of course. But don't you think you should make some friends in high places first?'

'Like who?' he asked.

'Hmm, let me see. How does Prince Bandar grab you?'

Afterword

Let me end by telling you how *The Diary of a Social Butterfly* came to be. In the 1990s when I was working at the *Friday Times* in Lahore, my editor asked me to think of a column that would appeal to women readers. 'Touching on issues of concern to women,' he said. 'Marriage, women in the workplace, raising children, women's health, you get my drift? But written with a light touch. Light, but not shallow.'

So I began writing a column about life as a single woman in Lahore. Called 'By The Way', it documented in as light and breezy a tone as I could manage, the travails and triumphs of my own life. But after two years I got tired of turning my own life inside out for the delectation of my readers and said as much to my editor. My editor was not pleased. The column had grown quite popular and he was unwilling to see it perish. In the end we reached a compromise: 'By The Way' could discontinue provided I found a substitute for it.

I spent the next couple of weeks trying to find a viable alternative to 'By The Way'. But whatever I wrote morphed into a weak imitation of it. I knew if I was to write anything at all original, I had to make a radical departure from that column. But how? With what?

Just about then I found myself at a very fancy, very big lunch party in Lahore, thick with prosperous business-*wallahs* and their stylish spouses. As I was helping myself to the buffet, I overheard a conversation between two ladies.

'So I bought this *shahtoosh* yesterday only,' purred a lady with rhinestone-encrusted dark glasses and diamond studs the size of rupee coins in her ears. Her ample torso was swathed in an eye-wateringly expensive shawl. 'I had four *shahtooshes* from before also but they were shorter. So I thought, never mind, no harm in getting one in seven yards also. After all, you only come to this earth once. So I got.'

'I *tau* don't wear shawls,' said the other, who was (almost) dressed in a teeny-tiny blouse that exposed acres of toned bare midriff and a slithery, whispery, crêpe sari. 'No offence, but wearing such a thick shawl, you know, makes one look a bit like an *ayah*, no?' She tossed her mane of blow-dried hair over her bare shoulder and looked pityingly at her stodgy lunch companion.

That was my eureka moment. I knew then that I would do a satirical column based on the lives of the rich and inane. But how was I to do it without naming names and making enemies? I needed a fictitious character who would not only be my mouthpiece but would also personify all the neuroses and insecurities to which people in her position are prey. Enter the Butterfly. But to highlight her silliness I needed a foil. Hence, Janoo. Janoo would need a family – The Old Bag, The Gruesome Twosome; and so would the Butterfly – Mummy, Aunty Pussy, Jonkers. They would have one child, Kulchoo, and live in Lahore. Janoo would be landed and educated, the Butterfly urban and foolish, and their marriage would be built on mutual misunderstanding. I had my column. Or at least the idea for it.

When I discussed it with my editor, he was luke-warm but allowed me, albeit grudgingly, to have a go. The column was an immediate success with my readers. It was new and yet familiar. It held a mirror up to them but was sufficiently good-humoured to cause no – or very little – offence. After two or three issues, it even won my editor over.

In the many years that I have been writing *The Diary of a Social Butterfly*, the question that I am asked most often is this: by whom is the central character inspired? I consider the query a compliment. For it means that my protagonist – the shallow, egotistical, obtuse Butterfly – is sufficiently credible for my readers to feel that she is based on a real person of my acquaintance. Though I often respond to the query with vague denials, the fact is that the Butterfly *is* based on someone I know intimately: myself.

The Butterfly is the embodiment of my own 'hidden shallows'. I may not speak or live like her. I may not have the same taste in clothes, music, film or for that matter, people. Nonetheless, the Butterfly is a true expression of my *Hello*-reading, self-absorbed, frivolous side, exaggerated manifold and unredeemed by any hint of self-doubt and unburdened by any desire for a more meaningful existence. Of course, I cannot claim to be the inspiration for all of her concerns and quests. I simply wouldn't have thought of them. So I borrow shamelessly from other people. When I hear of a particularly comic incident, I promptly cull it for the column. Many of the incidents described in this collection, such as the burglary where the burglars lectured their hapless victims on their unseemly dress, have really happened; not to me but to others. Many of the conversations relayed here I have overheard. And in reporting some of the scandals written up in the diary, I have once again crossed over from fiction to fact.

True to my original brief to address real-life issues, I have attempted to confront the concerns that govern the daily life of a character such as the Butterfly. Hence her preoccupation with political gossip, black magic, in-laws and money; holidays abroad, shopping, designerwear and money; domestic staff, BMWs, botox and money; society weddings, charity balls, scandals and money; property, Bollywood, divorce and money.

I have also tried to include in this column the bigger events of our times that have reverberated even in the life of one as sheltered as the Butterfly. So 9/11, the invasion of Iraq, the Kashmir earthquake, the tsunami, and 7/7, as they have impacted the Butterfly, have all been recorded in this diary. Moreover, the larger socio-political trends of recent years have also, I hope, been adequately reflected in the Butterfly's life: the face-off between civil society and the army, the rise of consumerism, the increasing cultural alienation of the rich, the gradual breakdown of law and order, the media revolution, women's growing presence in the workplace, the tension between landed gentry and new money, and the multifarious pleasures and pains of globalisation. So without ever intending to be, *The*

326

Diary of a Social Butterfly has become a record –
compiled admittedly by a rather cross-eyed observer –
of some of Pakistan's most turbulent years.

That is not to say that I have ever approached it as
a sociological treatise. With a protagonist as frivolous as
the Butterfly, there was only so much seriousness that
this column could reasonably accommodate. For me
it has been, and continues to be, great fun to write.
More than thinking up themes or creating situations
and introducing characters, I have enjoyed inventing
the language that has become the Butterfly's signature.
And in this effort Lahoris of my acquaintance have –
often unknowingly – helped hugely. On my own I
would never have been able to think up priceless
phrases like 'what cheeks!' Nor would I have had the
imagination to slip into a 'comma', to meet 'business
magnets' or get 'knocked up' by a truck. And I certainly
would not have laughed till I became 'historical'. For
this unintended largesse I thank my Pakistani friends,
relatives and acquaintances.

I owe another enormous thank-you to my sister,
Jugnu Mohsin, who, for all the years that I have been
living in London, cut off for the main part from the
comings and goings of Lahori society, has fed me the
priceless gems and nuggets that have allowed this
column to continue. Without her encouragement and

input it would have died long since. To my original editor, Najam Sethi, my gratitude for giving me the space and indulgence to begin this diary on the pages of his esteemed newspaper. Were it not for his persistent haranguing, it would never have been compiled into a book either. To my editor at Vintage, Victoria Murray-Browne, my thanks for her enthusiasm and patience. And for you, my readers, my heartfelt appreciation for keeping faith with the Butterfly. Which brings me to my final disclosure and the second most-asked question about this column: why does Janoo not ditch her? The answer, in all honesty, is: I don't know. Maybe one day he will.

Moni Mohsin
London, July 2008

www.vintage-books.co.uk